Melodra

Megan Parkinson

For Dad
The funniest, most supportive man I will ever know.
x

Copyright © 2023 Megan Parkinson All rights reserved

This book is a work of fiction. Names, characters, places, organisations, and incidents are either products of the author's imagination or are used fictitiously. Any resemblance to actual events, organisations, or persons, living or dead, is entirely coincidental and not intended by the author.

No part of this book may be reproduced, or stored in a retrieval system, or transmitted in any form or by any means, electronic, mechanical, photocopying, recording, or otherwise, without express written permission of the copyright owner.

Content Warnings: Melodramatic contains content that might be troubling to some readers, including, but not limited to, **strong language, mild descriptions of sex, death/illness of a parent** in regards to **cancer, PTSD** and **sexual assault**. Readers who are sensitive to these elements, please take note.

Cover design by: Kayla Coombs
Edited by: Lolli Molyneux
Audiobook Production: behear

9th November

Regretting life choices, specifically moving to London to become a 'successful' actor.

Well, today sucked. Not only did I trudge all the way across London for a dead-end audition, my bag got caught in the tube doors at Arnos Grove Station. Only after I screamed like a shagging fox did the doors release me and I fell arse over tit. Not my finest moment.

My audition? Is it even worth writing down? I showed up ten minutes early, as usual, only to be told they're running a 'tad' late. Which, in industry terms, means, "Get yourself comfy, love, you'll be here for a while."

Forty minutes rolled by, all the while I'm sat between two other auditionees. They had identical mousy-brown ponytails — clearly I'd missed the memo. My ginger frizz was drowning in dry shampoo and scraped back with a luminous pink headband. I must've looked wild in comparison. Both girls were also clearly prepubescent, their age (or lack of it) amplified by the fact their chaperone mothers were hovering around the room.

One of the mums — slightly weaselly-looking — cleared her voice in the way only very important people know how, "*ehem...*" and then proceeded to ask if my daughter had already gone in.

I could've died. I know I'm not a teenager anymore, not even close, but come on! I'm twenty-six, I don't look old enough to have a teenage daughter... Do I?

I felt like a fraud. A phoney. Like there was someone standing behind me with a megaphone screaming, "Yes, Mel is old! She's a fake! And she's wearing the last pair of clean underwear she owns because she couldn't be arsed to throw a load in the washer!"

I thought it couldn't have gotten any worse but then I was called into my audition. Met the assistant of the casting director's assistant and was asked what I thought of the script. I'd read it in length and wanted to say, "It's shite, Debora. Cliche at best, homophobic at worst, and the dialogue reads like it was written by a four-year-old."

But I want to make this month's rent so I lied and smiled and said, "Yeah, it's great! Loved it."

Then I was told to stand in front of the camera and heard three words I hate —

Use the space.

Ugh. Those words haunt most actors.

The scene is a girl asking a stranger for a lighter outside a club. How am I meant to use the space? It's a stationary scenario! Unless I mix things up a bit and chase the guy down the street for his lighter. I didn't, of course. No. Though because I was then panicking about 'using the space', I came across as a possessed lighter junkie desperate for a smoke.

I was swiftly told, "Thanks for coming in and we'll let you know."

If being in this industry has taught me anything, it's that they never let you know.

21st November

Woman unapologetically farted in my face on the escalator today. Didn't know how to respond.

Ian needs a new hobby. His online shopping obsession is now beginning to obstruct the front door. There's a big, heavy, obnoxious delivery propped up against the radiator in the hallway.

"It's a new wooden bed frame," he tells me, pulling at the stream of tape and jabbing a blunt pair of kitchen scissors into the cardboard.

"You haven't got enough money to buy a decent food shop, Ian. How have you managed to get a new bed frame?"

"On finance!"

"What was wrong with your old one?"

"It was metal. So, it released bad vibes into my body while I slept. That's why I was always waking up groggy and sick."

"That probably has more to do with the fact you use vodka as a sedative, Ian."

He ignored me and continued, "However, recent evidence shows wooden bed frames absorb bad toxins while you sleep so you wake up more invigorated."

"*Recent evidence*? You're having me on."

"No, seriously, I read about it on this sleep well blog."

Another hobby Ian needs to throw in the bin. Reading blogs that chat bollocks and have more adverts than word count.

My phone rang at that point. It was my Dad, calling from France. Moved there when Mum died, bought a vineyard and listens to Louis Armstrong's *Le Vie en Rose* on repeat. *It's what she would've wanted.*

"Freckles, I need you."

He sounded serious. Whether this was 'I've got my finger stuck in a plug socket again' or 'I've got a problem with my prostate' level of serious, I didn't want Ian to hear, so I scuttled off and hid in the bathroom.

"I don't know what I'm going to do, I really don't know what I'm going to do, Freckles. I want to be nice but I don't think I can take that many people—"

"I need context, Dad."

"Your cousin Willow is getting married."

There's a surprise. No, really, I'm shocked. The only part of marriage Willow has shown any interest in are the husbands of other brides. She's had numerous affairs with married men but nobody ever talks about it.

Tell a lie, Auntie Angela brought it up two Christmases ago when she drunk near enough three bottles of pinot. That was a fun Christmas.

"Who's the poor fella?"

"Gary or something."

"Does he have a divorce lawyer?"

"Willow has asked to hold the wedding here, at the villa. What am I supposed to tell her?"

"Tell her to piss off."

Dad tutted at me and I could feel him do his old man, disapproving head shake down the phone. I tried my hardest to think of an answer for him that wasn't oozing in sarcasm.

"Tell her you'd love to host the wedding—"

"What?"

"*However*, you'd feel uncomfortable with the idea that all her beloved friends and family will then need to foot the bill for hotels, plane tickets, travel, et cetera in order to share her special day with her. So wouldn't it be more appropriate for her to hold it somewhere closer to home?"

"But if she had it over there I'd have to buy all that stuff."

Says the man living on a French vineyard, I thought.

My phone beeped at me. It was my agent, Bethany Rollins. She never rings. Basically because she never has a reason to. Bless her, she's stuck with me through the dry and even drier years. If it weren't for the very successful actors on her client roster I would've been dropped yonks ago. But thankfully the famous lot get jobs that pay off her mortgage, and I occasionally get jobs that mean she can buy a nice new coat.

"Dad, can I ring you back?"

Regrettably I didn't give him time to answer, just hung up and switched calls. Bethany jumped right into it.

"You're an absolute bloody star, Mel. You really are!"

I laughed nervously, looking at my reflection in my toothpaste-spattered mirror. Too many freckles. Too much frizzy hair. Shit brown eyes staring back at me, and... *Is that jam on my chin?*

"Why? What have I done?"

"You've only gone and landed yourself a bloody movie!"

She didn't hear me scream as I dropped my phone into the toilet.

That reminds me — must add rice to the shopping list.

Ian had insisted we celebrate properly, so he did the ring round and before I knew it I was sitting in *Carlo's* with a plate of lobster ravioli in front of me.

Amarra had joined us. As she should. Best friend duty to show up and get pissed when called. She was sporting a pink cocktail umbrella in her hair for most of dinner.

Unfortunately, Tilly had also come along. We met at an acting class when I first moved to London seven years ago. How do I describe her? Picture the phrase, *'I've never had an orgasm in my life'* as a person, and you've got Tilly. Bit uptight, good looking but not the best personality in the world. Hell, who am I kidding? She's a bit of a bitch. Only invited because I fancy her brother.

Oliver, the brother in question, who for the first time in all the years I've known him was sitting next to me. *By choice.* He's regrettably one of those chiselled types, whose sole personality trait is going to the gym. Covered in tattoos, and hasn't had any relationship last longer than a traffic update. Not a deal breaker in my book.

Tilly had a monk on from the moment she sat down, fitting in her snide comments wherever she could. Her most notable quotes of the night?

"Do you think you'll actually manage to make it into the final edit of the film? Or get cut like you did in that period drama back in May?"

"I don't know why you bother auditioning for films, your features won't exactly come across well on a large screen. Your face is more built for the stage. Where the audience is sat far *far* away."

"Is anybody actually *interesting* going to be in this film? Or is it just nameless actors?"

Ian answered that one. "Well, I heard Jasmine O'Connell and Jack Hart are going to be in it."

Tilly had to hold back a yelp of horror.

"How'd you know that?"

Ian wiggled his phone at me. "Research, babe."

Tilly laughed a little too heartily, then nudged Amarra playfully, "Google chats so much rubbish, it says I'm twenty-nine!"

"You are twenty-nine," Amarra stated bluntly. She wasn't keen on Tilly either. Very much my best friend to a point where if I didn't like somebody, she didn't like them either, out of principle. No one would ever guess we'd only been mates for a year and a half. We'd met purely by fluke when assigned the same spot to hand out flyers for a new show. Hit it off immediately when she took a picture of us holding our cargo, emailed it off to the big boss to make sure we got paid, then dumped all of her flyers, and mine, into the nearest bin, and dragged me bowling. She is unlike any friend I've ever had.

Ian pulled up an article he'd saved onto his phone for just this moment.

"It says here, *'Symbol of Freedom'*, currently in pre-production, will begin filming in the New Year in Manchester. A dynamic script written by — *well, I can't pronounce that...* Oh, here we go. Starring three-time Academy Award nominee Jasmine O'Connell, as the brave *Atta Girl* Gabrielle Davis. And, *Violins in Vienna*'s very own Jack Hart as fighter pilot, Keith Meadows."

Tilly mimed a yawn. "Sounds like something you'd watch on the history channel when your teacher couldn't be arsed to teach."

"It sounds badass!" Oliver interrupted, leaning in to give me a squeeze. He didn't release his arm from my waist so his lips were right next to my ear. "So, are you going to be an *at it* girl, Mel? Fighting Germans? Wearing a sexy uniform?"

I think I kept it cool but I do distinctly remember snorting nervously at that point, like some giddy, horny, little piglet.

"No." Another nervous snort. "I'm playing Gabrielle's little sister."

"So you'll be playing right opposite, Jasmine!" Amarra couldn't have looked prouder. "She is wicked fierce."

Tilly rolled her eyes. "I've heard she's quite hard to work with."

"Aren't they all?" Ian mused. "Every successful actress has to have some streak of bitch running through her."

"Tilly would know."

"Piss off, Amarra."

I didn't pay attention to the rest of their bickering as Oliver's hand had slid down from my waist to the bottom of my spine.

"Don't go bitchy on us when you're famous, eh Mel?" he whispered in my ear before slowly moving his hand downward and briefly caressing my arse.

Oliver was coming on to me.

Well, either that or he's having a seizure.

18th December

After eating the contents of six advent calendars I can conclude my Christmas list to Santa consists of the following: 'Tampons and a new family'

Every year. EVERY BLOODY YEAR! I don't know why I do it to myself. I get the train back up to Yorkshire like an idiot and voluntarily attend the *'Fallon Christmas Clan Gathering'*.

Some bloke, can't remember his name, said something along the lines of, 'Insanity is doing the same thing over and over again and expecting a different result.'

That's what I do. Attend this shambles of a party expecting my family members to have gained some sort of empathy, or social etiquette, throughout the year, but no. They're all still as obnoxious and oblivious as the year before, without fail. And, if anything, some of them actually get worse.

It's Mum's side of the family so Dad never has to attend anymore. So for the fourth year in a row now, I'm enduring this crap on my own.

"Still no boyfriend then, Lil' Nips?" Cousin Willow asked, making a point of flashing her arrogantly large engagement ring at me.

Force a smile. Fake a laugh. Shove another cocktail sausage in your mouth.

Her newly acquired fiancé, Gareth, was more of a drip than I'd expected. Perfect prey for someone like Willow. Hanging around her like some obsessed puppy dog. He tried making conversation with me but Willow interrupted him at every turn. Taking every chance she could to talk about her sodding wedding.

Force a smile. Fake a laugh. Feign interest in centrepieces. Shove another cocktail sausage in your mouth.

"Saw you on the telly, Mel!" Uncle Kenneth said to me while he was wobbling out of the toilet, fly undone. "You didn't say anything, but I saw you! Is that the only job you got this year, or is this acting thing starting to pick up?"

"An acting career is nothing to be pursued, Melissa!"

Nana Tia is and always will be reigning queen of self entitlement and absentmindedness. She thinks she's all that but has a cardboard cutout of a questionable 60's pop star in her wardrobe.

"You should have been a midwife, Melissa. It's what your mum always wanted for you."

Ah yes. The dead mum guilt trip.

"Until she saw my science exam results, Nana."

"School was never really your thing was it, Mel?" Uncle Kenneth swirled his gin and tonic. "Too busy chasing boys!"

Auntie Angela, Nana Tia and three more of my cousins, including Willow, joined in at that point to discuss in length the exact point of my downfall. Was it my bone idle adolescence? The lack of interest in *real* school subjects? Or, in fact, was I to blame at all? As losing my mum makes many an excuse for me being a complete failure at life.

"You're never going to excel in life, Melissa, unless you really commit!"

"I'm committed to acting, Nana."

"It's not a proper job! You spend all your time going back and forth to these auditions that never go anywhere. You spend the rest of your time waitressing, *like that's a career*. You're sacrificing so much, and for what? Your mother would be turning in her grave."

I mean, we cremated her, but okay.

"I'm sorry, what am I sacrificing exactly?"

"Relationships," Angela chirped up. "You had that nice fella, what was his name? Franco? Felix? Ooo, it's on the tip of my tongue. Lanky lad — Mop of hair."

Willow unsuccessfully muffled a snigger with the back of her hand. "You mean Freddie, Mum!"

Freddie, God. My stomach churned. What a disaster of a relationship that was. Feels like years ago now. Hell, it was years ago... like a whole different life ago.

"Whatever happened to him?" Angela pushed, "We all thought we'd be buying a new hat with that one, what with you living together and all."

Nana Tia took me by the shoulder and sat me down, serious. "We have a room for you, Melissa. You can move back home, settle down. Kenneth's secretary is going on maternity leave soon, so you can have her job."

"She can?" Kenneth hiccuped.

"And before you know it you'll be back on your feet in no time."

I wanted to scream. Yell. Shout at the top of my lungs, "I am on my feet! I am successful. I have a job. A proper movie job! So will all of you just piss off!"

But I couldn't.

I didn't want them to ruin something I was actually quite excited about. If I brought up *Symbol of Freedom* now, they'd do nothing but stain it with their judgement and bullshit opinions. They'd break it down to dust, and blow it in my face. I'm always better off just saving myself the hassle and staying silent.

I hid in the upstairs toilet for the remainder of the party. Could hear Nana Tia shouting for me several times through the floorboards. It was only when I heard her shout for Gramps that I got my opportunity for an escape.

Grabbing my coat and car keys on the way, I purposely bumped into Nana Tia in the kitchen.

"Melissa, there you are! Have you seen your grandfather?"

"He's probably outside having a smoke. I'll go get him for you."

"Mmm, well, be quick. Angela's about to serve her trifle."

I bolted for the exit, hearing the words, "She's a lost cause that one," before slamming the back door behind me.

Grandpa Barry, better known as 'Gramps', was indeed having a smoke. Or at least trying to. Found him in the Christmas light-infested gazebo, on his hands and knees. "You alright, Gramps?"

"Lost me bloody lighter!" He looked up at me, an unlit ciggy lolling out the side of his mouth. "You gonna stand there like a Jehovah, or actually help me? Wahey!" He sprang upright clutching a lighter in his meaty paws. "Got the bugger."

With a few grunts and puffs he managed to get to his feet, before proceeding to collapse heavily onto one of the gazebo's benches.

"Wife's not wanting me is she?"

"'Fraid so."

"Balls." He lit his cig anyway. "Well I'll just have this one."

I sat beside him, mustering up my best Nana Tia impression. "Better make it quick, *Auntie Angela's about to serve her trifle.*"

Gramps laughed heartily. "That's uncanny that!" He elbowed me playfully. "You should be an actor!"

He let out a hefty puff of smoke.

"How *is* the acting gig going? You landed that next job yet?" He took my silence as the usual, *'No'*, then began to reassure me between a series of moist, phlegm-coated coughs. "It'll come, Mel. It'll come. As long as you're still enjoying yourself, then you take as long as you need to get there. It'll come."

"Tell Nana that."

"Pfft. She giving you a bit of a hard time?"

Understatement of the year, I thought.

"Just give her time, Mel."

"It's been years, Gramps. How long does she need?"

He took a deep drag. "Your Nana is very protective of you. It's not been long since your erm... mum died." He cleared his throat.

There was an unspoken rule that no one talked about Mum in front of Gramps. Her death had undeniably hit him the hardest. Reminded me of that quote: '*No parent should have to bury their child*' — again, not that we buried her. But 'no parent should have to set fire to their child' doesn't quite have the same ring to it.

For all his jokes and banter, Gramps never laughed anymore the way he used to with Mum. He didn't sing show tunes under his breath anymore either. He wasn't really himself anymore. *I don't think any of us are — try as we might.*

"You were home when yer mum were sick and it were nice having you here. But then in a flash you packed yer bags, went back off to London and it threw yer Nana. I think she feels responsible for you now, especially with yer Dad over the pond. She doesn't want to see you suffering. Wants what's best for ya', you know?"

I took a moment. "Do you think, *hypothetically,* if I did get a big acting job, Nana would accept what I do for a living and get off my case?"

Gramps chuckled to himself knowingly. "Probably not."

And that's what I didn't want to hear because I knew he was right. That's the problem with any sort of 'job' in the arts. No one around you sees it as a 'proper job' until you've *made it*. And even then, what constitutes 'making it'? You get one big film but you never get another. You didn't make it, you just got lucky. You get a series regular part in a soap for years, are a household name, retire successful. You won't be described as having 'made it' — more likely they'll say, 'Well you had a good innings but shame you never amounted to anything more.'

All anybody wants from you... *more*.

24th December

At what age does Christmas stop being magical and just become a financial strain and anxiety trigger?

You'd think, with online purchases being Ian's forte, that Christmas shopping would be his dream activity. But it's really not. He loves getting new stuff, don't get me wrong, but only for himself. When it becomes buying for somebody else, all of a sudden he's broke beyond measure and hasn't a clue where to go or what to buy.

"Serves you right for leaving it to the last minute," I told him as he fell through the front door, surrounded by plastic bags.

"I've had no money! I *have* no money! Therefore, I've now been forced to buy tat that'll all get thrown in the bin come Boxing Day anyway — *for God's sake!*"

One of his bags had gotten caught on the front door handle and when he tried to pull it free the bag had launched itself against the wall. We both heard a smash.

"Well, that's Mum's two-quid vase gone."

I would feel sorry for him but he's been like this the three years I've lived with him. He spends all of December moaning and groaning about how 'Christmas is a commercialised lie to get us to spend more money we don't have', yet come Christmas morning, he's giddy. Childlike. Desperate to open every present under the tree, even the ones that aren't his. He's pissed by noon, crying over the Christmas pudding, and singing carols to himself on the toilet.

I distracted him with chocolate and a brew.

"When does your dad's flight get in?"

Yep. Dad's actually coming over for the big day this year. Bringing presents and all. *Not Mum though, she's staying in France on the mantelpiece.*

"He's taken the train due to 'luggage reasons'. Which is basically code for 'I've got some stinky cheese for you'."

"Remind me again why he's coming here and we're not going to Le Chateau?"

"He doesn't have a chateau, Ian."

"It has six bathrooms."

"Neither of us can afford to go over there."

"I could scrape some cash together."

"Says the bloke who just bought and smashed his Mum's two-pound Christmas present." I pointed at the mountain of bags in the hallway. "That probably all amounts to less than twenty quid!"

Ian rolled his eyes. "Okay, so maybe I couldn't afford to go, but *you* — you're the one with the big movie job. What's your excuse?"

Damn. Dad still didn't know about my new job, and I wanted to keep it that way. How in the hell was I going to explain that to Mr Blabbermouth?

"What's the face for? You just started your period?"

I shook my head. "Can you maybe not mention anything about *Symbol of Freedom* to my Dad?"

"Why?" Ian asked, unmoved.

"Because he doesn't know about it."

"You haven't told him?"

"No."

"And *why not?*"

I wasn't able to put my finger on it. I didn't tell my family because they're dicks. With Dad, it was more like I wasn't telling him because he's the opposite. Dad's nice. *Really* nice and supportive and —

"I don't want Dad thinking this is something that it's not. He'll hear 'movie' and think I've finally got my big break."

"This could be your big break."

"And what if it's not?" I snapped. "Which, let's be honest, is more realistic."

Ian rolled his eyes. "God, a bit of optimism never hurt anyone, you know? It's Christmas, have a bit of faith."

Amarra has arrived with bottles of *very* nice red wine. *Is that bells ringing*? Nah — just the doorbell. It'll be Dad. Talk about busses... That doesn't look right. Buses? What's the pissing plural of bus? Buses? Busses? Busi? Bussy? No, definitely *not* bussy. Doorbell again — oh yeah, Dad. *Piss it.*

25th December

Happy Birthday Jesus.

I don't remember much of last night, not going to lie. A few blurry moments are there — like Dad showing up.

Dad gives the best hugs, particularly because he wears a vest, a shirt, a woolly jumper, a cardigan, and then a fleece jacket on top, no matter what the weather. Makes him very teddy bear-esque, and therefore incredibly huggable. I think Amarra went in for thirds after the takeaway arrived.

Food was eaten. A *lot* more was drunk. And after now seeing the mountain of wrapping paper under the tree I can confirm we opened all our presents.

It was after midnight so *technically* Christmas Day.

Ian got me a dress. I say, *'dress'* — it's more like a tea-towel.

"I got it in one of those charity shops in Muswell Hill. Four quid fifty. Absolute bargain!"

"I'm not surprised," I said, holding up a sliver of dark green fabric. "It's smaller than a fiver."

"Come on, you need more sexy clothes!"

"I'm not prepared to argue that, Amarra. Especially in front of my Dad."

Though, I'd have nothing to argue either way. Amarra was right. My wardrobe consists of oversized jumpers, leggings, and slipper socks. There's no thongs (for good reason too, they're uncomfy as hell! Mum used to call them butt floss). I've no mini skirts, no crop tops, and no skimpy, backless dresses... *Until now.*

Amarra gave me a "Love Yourself", eye-wateringly bad, bath set. A self-care book that had a big, happy, naked woman on the front, and when my Dad's back was turned, a new vibrator. *I think she's trying to tell me something.*

Dad (**drum roll**) got us all smelly cheese and bottles of his own wine. Surprise, surprise.

"Bet you were popular on the train, Mr Bishop!" Amarra giggled.

"There were a few complaints," Dad owned up sheepishly. "But, in fairness, I don't think I was the only one contributing to the smell."

"Must be so nice living in France, getting to eat this stuff all the time." Ian held his Brie close to his nose and inhaled deeply. "I'd be so fat."

Dad remembered at that point he had something else for me. Not a present as such, just the worst thing he could've possibly given me ever.

Wedding invitation.

Dad shuffled in his chair uncomfortably. "I told Willow I'd pass it along, save on stamps."

"You've seen, Willow?"

Then it hit me. He's letting her host her damn wedding at his villa. *Coward.*

I read aloud, "Willow Fallon and Gareth Price would like to invite Melissa and guest — *a plus-one?* She's given me a bloody plus-one? That cow bag!"

"Isn't a plus-one a good thing?" Amarra asked, leaning over my shoulder to take a good look at the invitation herself.

"You'd think! But Willow's only done it because she knows I've got no one to bring!" I shoved the invitation between the sofa cushions. "This means I've got to bloody find someone!"

Ian waved his hand in front of my face, mouth full of cheese. "Err, hewwo?!"

"I mean a date."

"I can be a date!" Ian continued, bolting up to plead his case, sloshing the last of his wine down his front. "I can pretend to be your boyfriend if it means going to Le France!"

"Willow knows you're my housemate, Ian, and not to mention gay."

"You're gay, Ian?" Dad asked, adjusting his glasses. "I didn't know that. I don't think I've ever met a gay."

"Dad—"

"I've always wondered, and can finally ask now I've got one in front of me, how do you do it?"

Ian went pink and Amarra almost fell off the sofa laughing. I was mortified.

"*Dad!*"

In his innocence, he hadn't realised what he'd said, or how it sounded. Until he did, and then he started to stutter and shuffle like he had a firecracker up his arse.

"I didn't mean. Oh, Ian. I meant in this day and age with society being so prejudiced, not '*it*' as in sex. I mean, I know how you would do sex — that is, I can imagine. Never had first-hand experience. Can I say that? 'Hand' experience? Or does that sound like I've—"

Can clearly see why that memory is burned into my brain despite the haze of wine. God, my head. Maybe it's time to buy a wooden bed frame? Have my toxins absorbed. *Oop, I think I can hear Ian vomiting into the toilet.*

Ha! Maybe I'll just keep the bed I've got then.
Merry Christmas.

5th January

New Year's Resolutions. Why do we make them? Seriously.

Going to start a new acting job is kind of like waiting in line for a big, scary rollercoaster. You're nervous, excited, and yet can't shake off the notion that if this goes horribly wrong you could die.

Production sent a car to pick me up this morning at God-knows-what o'clock. So now, I'm sitting in a barren Heathrow Airport, with duty free closed, staring at a departures board. Thrilling stuff.

It's ridiculous really — A flight up to Manchester Airport. I could've quite easily just taken the train. But no, production was insistent. It's cheaper apparently*!*

The flight was *eventful*. No, we didn't crash into the sea and have to live out our days on an uncharted island. No, there weren't snakes or a hostile takeover — thank God. However, there *was* a little old lady in my seat. She insisted it'd take her the whole flight just to stand up again, so would I mind swapping?

Didn't think too much of it until I realised I'd swapped my economy, no-leg-room chair, for her business-class, free-breakfast seat. *I'm going to hell for this.*

"First-time flyer?" the woman next to me asked, as I craned my head over the back of my chair for the ninth time. "There's really nothing to be afraid of."

Not afraid, just having a moral crisis, love, I thought.

"Oh, I fly all the time."

I say 'all the time' — in reality it's once a year, maximum. And it's only ever to see my dad. I fly over for quality time that's supposed to last a week but it's always, without fail, cut short by Bethany ringing me up:

"You've got an audition in Holborn tomorrow morning. Great part. Can you make it?"

I'm supposed to reply with, "I'm sorry, Bethany, but I'm in France with my darling dad, who I've not seen for ten months. We're trying desperately to get a tan, but both being ginger, failing badly. Tell casting they can either see me when I get back or miss out on me all together, their loss. Got to go now, croissant time! *Au revoir*!"

But I don't, do I?

I immediately spiral. Think: 'This could be the next job! Can't miss it! Must make this audition at all costs!'

There's a manic rush to pack. I spend money I don't have on an extortionately-priced last-minute flight back. Beg my dad for forgiveness and before I know it I'm back in London after only a day away. I don't sleep because I spend all night learning lines, and then quick as a flash, I'm in front of a casting director's assistant with baggy eyes, sunburnt cheeks, and unkempt hair. Never get the job, *obviously*. Because who'd want to hire that hot mess?

"Today we'll be flying from London Heathrow to Manchester."

The woman beside me was rummaging through her purse. "Seriously, if it's the take-off that's bothering you, I have some mints in my bag."

"What for?"

"I always find flying easier when you've got something to suck on."

"Oh yeah?" I mused to myself. "How hot is the pilot?"

Oh God, I said that out loud, didn't I?

I sunk into my seat ready with a swarm of apologies before I realised the woman was in hysterics. Both hands over her mouth trying not to burst out with laughter. Then—

"Fuck. You're Jasmine O'Connell."

I just made a blow-job joke in front of a three-time Academy Award nominee.

Her eyes went a little wide, her mood suddenly shaken by my outburst. She shuffled ever so subtly away from me.

I don't blame her. I was staring.

"Sorry, I just..." I blinked, dumbly. "I don't know how to recover from this."

"What?"

"I'm your sister. Not like in a soap opera way. Just in a *Symbol of Freedom*, Melissa Bishop way. Hello."

It was Jasmine's turn to stare.

Then, *BOOM!*

"Oh my God, *you're* Melissa?! I've heard so much about you!" She leaned across the arm rest separating us and gave me a squeeze. She smelled like orange juice. "I've been begging the office to give me your number so I could call you and introduce myself before it all kicked off but I lost the chance."

"Please switch off all laptops and store them securely in the overhead lockers for take-off and landing."

"Catherine said you absolutely nailed your audition. She said you 'were a rite funny lass'. I should've known!"

"Would you mind putting your tray up? Thank you."

"I had a feeling you might be on this flight, but it would've been a bit weird if I'd gone up and down the cabin trying to find you. Can you imagine? Me, going to every woman on the plane, 'Excuse me, are you about to be my sister?'"

"Please feel free to now walk about the cabin."

"So, how are you feeling about it all? I've tried to do some research but when the script is such a combination of real events and fiction it's tricky, you know? And I don't know what the production team are on. I've had nine edits since last Monday, not including the two emails I got last night that I daren't look at."

"Can I interest either of you in some tea or coffee?"

"Not for me, thank you. Are you staying at the Grand Hotel? Or round the corner? I like to be where they put everyone else. Hate being on my own. Did this one job and I was in a different place entirely to the rest of the cast! They'd all been put up in a hotel, able to have dinner together, drinks, laughs, and I'm being driven twenty minutes in the other direction to the middle of nowhere! Because they thought I would want somewhere nicer! What's nice about eating by yourself?"

"We will shortly be landing in Manchester. Please return to your seats."

Holy crap, Jasmine O'Connell doesn't shut up. Like it bothers me! She was speaking to me. *Me!* And not because a script had told her she had to.

Almost can't believe I'm writing this, but I'm going to dinner with Jasmine O'Bloody Connell. At least I'm supposed to be. I don't quite know how it's going to happen now I'm sitting in my hotel room with no way to contact her. Don't have her phone number. Don't have her room number. Bloody hell.

It's not going to happen, is it? Jasmine will probably get room service. I'll wander across the road for a meal deal and sit in my room watching trash TV thinking about what might have been.

I should've asked for her room number, not just got off the lift at my floor. But I was nervous and she wouldn't stop talking. Seriously, I know more about Jasmine than I probably do about Ian at this point. She's an only child. Her dad is an executive producer, not that it's affected the trajectory of her career — *yeah right*. She loves food markets and spoken word nights. She's trying to take up crochet but just can't find the time. She's a Leo, thinks diet culture should be illegal, is allergic to nuts and shellfish — and what else? Oh, yeah, she hates her new fringe.

I know Jasmine's somewhere up in the high heavens of the hotel. She's probably in a suite or something. Does this hotel even have suites? I've never seen a suite, let alone been in one. There's probably pictures of a suite in the information book. Let's have a nosey.

There's someone knocking on the door.
Where's the 'Do not disturb' sign gone?

I found Jasmine in the hallway looking a little lost. "I thought I'd misremembered your room number from when we checked in," she laughed nervously. "Still on for dinner, or—?"

"Yeah, course!" I blurted out, a bit too eager. "Just need to change."

Into what? I screamed internally to myself.

"Oh, fab. Okay." She squeezed past me and into my room. It was basically a bed in a cupboard, with an ensuite the size of a shoe box attached. Jasmine placed her designer handbag on the mattress runner, then perched herself elegantly beside it.

"I'm not really the strip-tease type, but alright. Come on in. I'll whack some music on and do my best."

Jasmine's face flooded with horror.

"I'm sorry," she yelped. "I should've just waited in the hall!"

I raised my hands to stop her from leaving. "I'm kidding. Chill. Sit back down, I'll change in the bathroom."

I grabbed my nicer clothes from my suitcase (still a top and leggings, but at least these didn't have holes in the crotch).

"I'm so sorry," Jasmine said again through the bathroom door. "I'm not very good at this."

"Not good at what?"

"This! Starting a new job. Meeting new people..."

I stepped out, one shoe not yet on. "Could've fooled me, sis."

6th January

Note to self: After eating a 12-inch garlic chicken pizza, brush EXTRA hard before bed.

Last night feels like a dream. Constantly wondering if it happened. All Jasmine and I did was eat food and chat. The conversation wasn't even that thrilling, just trivial stuff. But I was talking with somebody famous, *really* famous. Not that she acted like it. Tilly had drilled the rumours about Jasmine's diva-ish behaviour into me before I left. Like yelling at runners for giving her regular milk rather than almond. Getting costume designers fired for dressing her in unflattering colours. Snapping a boom mic clean in half because it had gotten too close to her face.

    I thought back to last night when Jasmine could barely pluck up the nerve to ask the waiter for some tomato sauce. Found myself shaking my head, amused. Tilly had clearly been having me on.

"You couldn't have got your lines more perfect if you tried," I reassured Jasmine, passing back her script. Despite this, she continued to pace nervously around her tiny trailer of a dressing room. It wasn't luxurious like I'd expected, but plain, plastic, and smelling like your average camper van.

"You seem pretty calm for a first day on set," Jasmine noted, crumpling up today's call sheet and sides into her pocket.

"Oh, I've met you. Scary bit's over for me now."

Jasmine's eyes narrowed. "You think I'm scary?"

I chuckled again, tomato sauce coming to mind. "No, definitely not."

"Well, that's nice to hear." Jasmine wrinkled her nose playfully. "You're not scary either."

"Oh, I don't know about that. You haven't seen me act yet."

No one made a good first impression today. The director, *Andrew Dale* — first thoughts? Bit of a wanker. He keeps doing this weird judgemental pout when he's giving notes, and referring to me as 'you'. I don't know if he's trying to establish dominance, or he genuinely has no idea who I am, or what my name is.

"You. I need you sat at the table. Fast as you can."

I tried not to give him the finger and just sat where I was told. Jasmine arrived on set with one of the runners hovering so close he almost tripped her up.

"Jasmine!" Andrew cheered, open armed. "Right, quick chat about the scene. We've moved a bit of the dialogue about—"

Jasmine's face fell.

"Just a few words swapped here and there, nothing major. Now, if we do a line run with—"

"*Melissa.*"

"Yes, you. Maybe we can get these changes into your pretty little head, and then start shooting, hmm?"

Cross out *'bit of a wanker'.* Replace with 'massive wanker.'

The rest of the morning was spent sat at that God-awful table cringing every time the script supervisor came over to *'correct'* Jasmine on another line mistake or continuity error.

"You lifted your hand just a fraction too early. And you lean onto the table at the start of the line: *'If I were to meet a man who...'* rather than at the end. Also, Andrew has asked that you try—"

"I need a minute," Jasmine suddenly said, placing her head in her hands wearily. "Like, some air."

She headed straight for the fire exit despite Andrew's protests.

"Jasmine, we have a break scheduled in twenty minutes!"

The door slammed shut, leaving the entire set uncomfortably silent.

"And so it begins," Andrew muttered under his breath, sitting back at his monitor.

The first AD, Benjamin, took a step in my direction. "You might as well take five too, Mel. I don't know how long Jasmine will be."

I shrugged. "She said a minute." I gave Andrew a wicked smile. "I mean, we all waited forty minutes for camera B to get its shit together — what's sixty seconds for Jasmine to do the same, eh?"

It was a *long* minute, but eventually the fire door did clunk back open. Jasmine returned to her mark, her eyes a little puffier, but nothing a makeup check couldn't fix.

"Right," Jasmine took a deep breath. "What was it you wanted me to try, Andrew?"

He began flicking through his notes, agitated. While he was occupied, I leant over the table and squeezed Jasmine's hand.

"You all good, sis?"

Her eyes looked almost translucent. "Yeah, first-day nerves getting the better of me. I feel like I can't breathe."
"That'll be the dress," I teased. "Makes your tits look good though."

Jasmine let out a half-exhausted laugh then smiled, thankful.

Before I knew it, Benjamin bellowed for the entire set to be quiet and Jasmine was reeling off lines; in the right order, with her hands moving at exactly the right times. The clapper board was snapped shut for an end board, and we were 'moving on to the next scene'.

Just got off the phone with Amarra. Didn't realise she was at work, and I was happy to call back, but she wanted to know everything, and 'stat'. So she's just been hiding from her prick boss, Danny, round the back of the club between the wheelie bins.

"Jasmine managed to keep it together for the rest of the day, but God, everyone was on her case," I told her, "I might as well have not even been there. No one really spoke directly to me, except for Jasmine and the first AD—"

"AD?"

"Assistant Director. Benjamin is like the big boy on set with the earpiece and the radio. He's in charge of everything. He started to be more understanding as the day went on, but if anything Jasmine just got worse."

"She flip her lid?" Amarra prodded, eagerly.

"No, I mean, she looked like she was going to pass out. To be fair, that many crew members crammed into a box set, while you're squished into a dress that's deliberately two sizes too small, and told you're getting your lines wrong every other take, I'd be the same."

"God, that sounds horrendous. Tilly will be disappointed."

"Why?"

"She's been counting on Jasmine being such a bitch that you quit."

"Ha! I don't think Jasmine's got a malicious bone in her body, Mar. Though I can understand how her anxiety could come across as difficult to work with. I can't even imagine the pressure she's under."

"Sounds like she's doing her best."

"At least she's doing something. I'm just sat there, doe-eyed!"

"And getting paid for it. I know which role I'd prefer..." Amarra trailed off, the line going quiet.

"Everything okay with you?" I queried, realising I'd rambled on about myself and not even thought to ask.

"Oh, I'm fine," Amarra cleared her throat. "Landlord's being a dick, as usual. Brother is back on the sofa, as Mum and her new fella have kicked him out. Oh, and I smashed my phone screen."

"Jesus, Mar. That sounds awful, why didn't you say anything?"

"It's fine, Mel. Don't worry about it." Amarra suddenly laughed heartily. "Oh, and err... Oliver has been asking about you."

"Give over!"

"Yeah, he came into work yesterday for a couple of drinks with his gym mates, said he wants to hear from you when you get back from Hollywood."

"That's an interesting development..."

Amarra hummed in agreement, before informing me, "You do know that if you shag him Tilly will never speak to you again?"

I laughed. "And that's supposed to put me off, is it?"

9th January

Being star-struck doesn't last long when you realise most 'famous people' are dicks.

Fourth day filming. Today didn't start well. In fact, it didn't start at all. I was put into a car with driver Dermot, only ten minutes after arriving.

"We're going to have to move your scene to tomorrow, Mel," the 2nd AD, Carrie, apologised. "We're just not going to get everything done today. Is it alright if we send you back to the hotel?"

Like I have a choice, I groaned in my head.

I got into the car, feeling *very* sorry for myself. I'd spent all morning waiting for pick-up. I'd done at least 5,000 steps around my bed, 200 star jumps *on* my bed, and watched hours of stupid daytime TV, counting down the seconds. All that only to be fobbed off upon arriving. Absolute bollocks.

Carrie knocked on the windscreen while yelling, "Just one more for you Dermot before you set off. They're just finishing up in costume!"

Dermot replied with something incoherent. He's Irish, and his accent is unbelievably thick. I've sat in the back of his car for an accumulation of about six hours during the last four days. We've had numerous conversations and I haven't understood a single one of them. Embarrassingly, it's all been guess work.

The back passenger door beside me swung open and I was blinded. A silhouette, large and overbearing, stared down at me, sunlight pouring in from behind.

"I'll go around."

The door slammed shut, and then the sound of heavy footsteps on gravel traced around the back of the car. It gave me the chills, like I was partaking in a thriller movie. Specifically the bit where the beast is circling the tent, only in the next moment to rip a side open and devour the closest character.

Dermot gave me a knowing wink in the rear view mirror. Then the opposite door opened and into the back of the car collapsed *Jack Hart*.

"All ready, Mr Hart?" I think Dermot asked. To be honest, all I heard was, *'Tall braided measure arse'*, but considering context, I'm definitely going to go with him actually saying the former.

Jack grunted, "Yes", never looking up from his phone.

Dermot revved up his engine and off we went in heavy silence.

Jack's phone kept pinging, flashing, buzzing. A continuous flurry of texts, emails, and notifications. My phone was basically dead. *Like my social life, clearly.*

It occurred to me as we joined the motorway that Jack was willingly ignoring me. It wasn't as if he'd sat beside me never looking up from his phone and just not seen me. He had seen me. Looked directly at me, made a conscious decision not to sit on my lap, and now deemed me unworthy to speak to. This epiphany pissed me off, to a point where the part of my brain that causes me the most trouble started to talk — despite the rest of my brain's objections.

"As much as I hate small talk there's really no way around it. Unless you actually enjoy awkward silences in the back of a car with a stranger? Which is fine if you do, but personally I find it a bit shit."

Jack's head turned to face me in slow motion. He blinked.

"What?"

"I was just saying, it's quite a random situation we find ourselves in. Thrown together like this. Do you want to chat, or do you actually prefer silence?"

Blink. "*Sometimes.*"

"Is this one of those times? Or do you think you could manage a bit of small talk? It'll make the drive go quicker."

"...Small talk?"

"Yeah, like what do you think of the weather? Isn't it nice? Or hell, let's get personal, what's your favourite colour?"

Blink.

"Grey."

Mother of God. I thought. *Did he just say 'grey?'*

I think that told me everything I needed to know about Jack. One word. One answer to a silly question and already I can deduct he is unimaginative, bland, and dull. Because whose favourite colour is *fucking grey?*

Doubt very much he'd have been labelled 'World's Fourth Sexiest Man' if all those voters had known his favourite colour. They would have overlooked his undeniable good looks. His dirty blonde hair, luscious green eyes, smooth chiselled jaw, and just said, 'Yeah, he's fit, but his favourite colour is grey, Susan, so that's a no from me.'

"What's yours?"

"What's my what?"

"Favourite colour." Jack slipped his still-beeping phone into his pocket. "Or should I ask the driver first, let you have time to think, since it's such a poignant question?"

Didn't take a genius to tell he was taking the piss.

"Dermot," I said, sharply. "*The driver* is called Dermot."

Jack's brow furrowed as he turned fully to face me. "Hmmm. And what are you, crew?"

"Cast... *actually*." I forced a smile. "I'm playing Gabrielle's little sister."

Jack's eyes widened momentarily. "Jesus, for a minute there I thought you were going to say you were playing Gabrielle!"

Who knew Director Andrew would have competition for biggest wanker? A response that extreme at just the thought of me playing his love interest? It's insulting. No doubt he was sitting there thinking I'm not famous enough. Not fit enough. Probably not fit at all compared to all of his previous co-stars.

"I don't remember Gabrielle having a sister in the script."

My jaw clenched. "It's kind of integral to the plot that she has a sister. Seriously, how have you missed that?"

Jack shrugged. "I've not had time to read the whole thing."

Translation: I've read my stuff and thought 'sod that' to reading anything involving somebody else.

Jack cleared his throat. "Was today your first day?"

"No, I started about four days ago."

"I don't technically start till next week."

"Then why are you here?"

That came out bitchier than intended. I couldn't help it, he'd pissed me off. The Gabrielle comment had rubbed me completely the wrong way, and I couldn't shake it. I wanted out of the car. Was even considering just opening the side door and rolling out into oncoming traffic. Would've been less painful than the conversation.

"I had a day free from *Violins* and they needed me for a costume fitting."

A mischievous idea flickered through my mind. Amarra would always play dumb with guys who were rude just for the hell of it. I never really understood it but Jack was just too smug, too brooding, and too self-obsessed to let the opportunity to irk him go.

"What's *Violins*?"

Jack's face fell, just a little. His genuine surprise reassured me of everything I'd assumed about this arrogant prick from the moment he fell into the car.

"*Violins in Vienna*. It's a TV show." His eyebrows twitched, his eyes scanning my face, looking for the wind up. "Quite a big show, actually."

"Oh," I shrugged. "Never heard of it. But, ya know, good for you."

I *have* heard of it. Of course I have. It's hard not to without being a member of one of those 'untouched by civilisation' colonies. *Violins in Vienna* is one of the biggest, if not *the* biggest show on at the moment. You can't get through London without seeing Jack, half naked, posing with a violin, on the side of a double decker bus. It's one of those period dramas where the blokes wear top hats and britches, and the women all blush and swoon. It's filled with all the good stuff: sex, murder, scandal, and *of course* more sex. Ian's favourite show, *obviously*, but not my cup of tea. I prefer old biddy quiz shows.

"Anything you've been in that I would've seen?" Jack asked, throwing a curveball into the conversation.

I felt my cheeks grow hot. The only reply coming to my mind was, '*Well, not to brag but I was in a toothpaste advert last Christmas. My teeth were the 'before' shot'.*

"Nope," I replied instead. "Don't think so."

Jack smirked triumphantly, which set my blood boiling.

Ding-ding-ding! We have a wanker winner!

"But I've got a couple of work opportunities on the horizon," I lied. *Unless I can count being promoted to pot washer and Christmas elfing at the local garden centre as 'work opportunities'?*

"Same," Jack nodded along. "Though more theatre, thank God. I'm getting tired of being on set. Theatre isn't as good for the career but I really feel the need to get back in front of a live audience, you know?"

"Yeah?" I humoured him.

I hated doing theatre. Going to see it? Love it. Maybe even writing for the stage some day: ideal. But acting for the theatre? Torture. TV and film are so much easier. With theatre, yes, it has its charms. Rehearsals are gruelling but with the right cast they can be a lot of fun. You have the thrill of being in front of an audience, true, but only if people actually buy tickets. And even then, you can end up with a bunch of school kids on the front row, who heckle, throw food on the stage, cheer at the end, as if Shakespeare's *Romeo and Juliet* is suddenly panto and somehow Juliet stabbing herself is on par with Widow Twankey tripping over a paint bucket.

"I'm even considering doing something that's not the West End. Something really intimate. Like when there's only a hundred people in the audience or something. I think it will really help me reconnect with my craft."

I stifled a laugh with the back of my hand. I thought I'd caught it but Jack shot me a questionable glare.

"I'm sorry," I apologised insincerely. "You sound like you've just been birthed by a top drama school."

"You say that like it's a bad thing," Jack's eyebrows furrowed.

"To some people it is," I let out a full laugh. "I mean, you all come out of drama school filled to your eyeballs with Stanislavski and Pinter, and a bunch of classical playwrights who've had maybe one good play and the rest that followed mediocre at best. You spend three years being told breath technique will get you the job. When really it's your mum having gone to school with the executive producer. And you're paying for the privilege to be taught by could-have-been actors who are so resentful of an industry that didn't want them they're willing to build up the hopes of every sodding cannon fodder young actor waiting in line. And those teachers will smile smugly as each hopeful student, inevitably, crashes and burns. Unless, of course, one of their students is the exception to the rule. Which, I imagine, was you? That one, working-class, usually northern, student who has that little bit of instinct that makes them stand out at their end-of-year showcase. First to be signed with a big, shiny agent. And, proudly, your drama school can write all over their website about their stunning successful alumni, forgetting to mention the ones who left crippled by student debt, no agent, and a nine-to-five job in an office."

From Jack's slack-jawed expression I could assume I'd just hit that nail on the head. I wonder which school he belonged to?

"I'm guessing you never went to drama school then..." Jack finally said, in a mildly judgemental tone. "Was that by choice or just because you *couldn't* get in?"

Now that wasn't mild at all, *that was full-blown judgemental.*

I turned my attention to Dermot, the urge to throw myself out of the car more appealing with every passing second. "Do you think you could drop me off in town, Dermot? I fancy a walk and some food that isn't room service."

"Sure thing, Mel."

"Mel?"

I couldn't explain it but hearing Jack repeat my name made my throat close up and my inner thigh tingle. My cheeks burnt hot with embarrassment — reacting like that just because he said my name? Ugh. He said it out loud in a rusky, sexy, gravelled tone just to piss me off even more.

Fuck this for a game of soldiers.

"And you are?"

He smiled. "Call me Jack."

14th January

What can I say about hotel stays? Other than the fact I always seem to be put in a room adjacent to a couple, who are too drunk, too loud, and too eager to have sex.

It's my first *official* day off. Just a day. No biggy. I can find something to do. Easy. How many times have I wanted a whole day to myself at home? I could read a book. Catch up on some correspondence. Maybe even do some writing — *real writing*, I don't just mean this. I could really make good use of my time today, and for once in my life be proactive.

 Bored. Bored. Bored. Bored. Bored.
 TV doesn't have enough channels.
 I've got to get out of this room, I feel as though I've been sectioned.

 Getting out of my room was a good idea for about twenty minutes. I felt high on non-hotel room air while taking a walk about. I got lost pretty quickly, every road looks the same! A Mancunian would probably say the same about London to be fair.
 I talked myself out of buying Ian a tacky souvenir before eventually finding myself outside a cake café. The window display was calling out to me, and when cake calls, I answer.

The door to the café had a little bell above it that jingled announcing your arrival. Though as it went off, no one from behind the counter looked at me. Three girls, all in a tight circle, were tittering by the coffee machine.

I'm British, so, naturally, I didn't say anything, or walk out — just endured the poor service, waiting to be acknowledged.

"Sorry, didn't see you there. What can I get for you?"

The other two girls continued to giggle and whisper, every now and then popping up from their huddle like giddy meerkats.

"Just a breakfast tea, and a lemon drizzle cake, please."

"Sure. Take a seat and we'll bring it over."

I went for the window. Might have looked odd, not getting out a laptop or book, but I liked to people-watch, as Mum used to call it.

'Observe the silliness of life and remind yourself what you're momentarily a part of'.

She never said that.

Mum was never that philosophical about it. Mum would've said, 'I like her coat, do you think she'd do a swapsies?' or 'Oop, OAPs on tour. How many do you think will make it to the end of the day? The chances aren't looking good for the one at the back with the walker, that's for sure."

I laughed to myself.

"Something funny?"

I almost jumped out of my seat.

Sat opposite me, without having made a sound, was Jack. I wouldn't have recognised him if it weren't for the smirk. He'd had his blonde hair cut short at the sides but left slightly longer on the top. Definitely more fitting for a pilot than the style he'd had before. He looked cleaner and sharper, but still held himself like a smug knobhead.

"*Jesus.*"

"No, just me. Hello, you."

Another prick who refers to me as 'you'. Bloody perfect.

I shook my head. "Sorry, do I know you?"

Jack grinned, amused. "We met in Dermot's car last week," he said. "Mel, isn't it?"

Poof. There went my cheeks again because he said my name aloud. I needed to regain control of the situation before he started to think he was making me blush. "Sorry, yes. Hello. Good to see you again, John."

His smile vanished, and his face turned sour. "It's Jack, actually."

Before I could reply, a rattling cup of tea on a saucer was placed down in front of me, then my cake, then a fork. I looked up at all three quivering waitresses, whose eyes were all completely fixed on Jack.

It finally made sense: bad service because there was someone famous in the building. *Good God.*

The one on the left had a wobbling bottom lip, and looked like she might cry.

"Is there... err... anything else?" The middle one sounded like she was buffering. "I mean, can we get you anything else? If you're staying? Maybe? Please?"

I wanted to slap her. Shout, 'Get a grip woman! You're letting the side down!'

No wonder Jack has an inflated ego with this kind of thing going on around him.

"I'll have another black coffee," Jack ordered, without looking directly at any of them. For some reason his eyes were remaining fixed upon me.

There was a muffle of, "Of course", "Right away", "I'll get that for you," and then a scuttle back to the coffee machine like a huddle of chattering seagulls.

I rolled my eyes. Okay, I may have stumbled and got red in the face a couple of times with Jack but at least I haven't been that bad. *Bloody embarrassing.*

"Ignore them," Jack mumbled to draw back my attention. "Enjoying your day off?"

"Yeah, it's been good," I lied, emptying two sachets of sugar into my tea.

"I'm starting today," Jack inhaled deeply, puffing out his chest. "My pick-up is in about an hour, so I'm just trying to kill some time. Not think about it, you know?"

I sipped my tea. Almost burned my mouth but I didn't know what else to do. I was sat in a café, in

Manchester, with Jack Hart. There wasn't a 'go-to' procedure in my brain for this kind of thing.

His coffee was placed down in front of him, then a napkin, then a fork. "Just in case you were sharing the cake."

There was a trio of giggles. All three waitresses were looking at me, then at Jack, then at me again, like we were playing bloody tennis for them.

"Err, thanks." Jack handed them a fiver, told them to keep the change, and with a dismissive waft of his hand, off they scurried.

Was that how he always presented himself? He did something similar with Dermot. Never a goodbye, just a limp-wristed waft. Probably thinks he's some sort of royal. He gets treated that way by us 'general public', so it wouldn't surprise me.

"I'm looking forward to it, don't get me wrong. I've been eager to start but it's a big scene. I have a lot of big scenes, but today's is tricky."

Was Jack aware he was still talking?

"And I like World War Two stuff. Plus, it's a nice change from *Violins*, as that's more—" he slapped the table, "Oh, sorry, I forgot *you* don't know what *Violins* is!"

"Pretty sure it's an instrument," I replied before picking up my fork.

He laughed, then took a sip of his coffee before telling me I'd "have to watch it some time. Download a few episodes when you get back to your hotel room. Let me know if I'm any good."

Then he winked at me.

Jesus.

I shoved a large portion of cake into my mouth and used chewing as an excuse for my lack of reply. This man was infuriating. I knew I was mistaking his sleaze for charm, and that in itself was beginning to fry my brain.

Jack looked around the café, bored. "So, what do you think of Jasmine?" he asked, fixing his eyes back on me. "You've done enough scenes with her to form a strong enough opinion."

I shrugged. "She's nice."

"And?"

"And talented."

"Okay. And what do you think of Andrew?"

Cake crumbs were starting to get lodged in my throat, the lemon drizzle welding my teeth together.

"He's thorough."

"Think the film will turn out well?"

I shrugged again. "Not for me to say."

Jack bit his lip and I felt my whole face go numb. "Have I done something wrong?"

Debatable, I thought.

"Because I'm a bit stumped as to where the chatty Mel has gone."

I laughed, uncomfortable. "You've asked questions. I've answered. That's chatting isn't it?"

Jack leaned onto the table, drank some more of his coffee and chuckled.

"When we first met, not that you remember it, you talked your head off. Chatted about favourite colours, small talk, drama school... I took you for some bubbly, opinionated, sort of social chatterbox. And now I can't so much as get a full sentence out of you." He leaned even closer. "Why?"

I racked my brain for an answer, eventually sputtering out, "First impressions can be deceiving."

He raised an eyebrow and softly smirked. "And what was your first impression of me?"

You're a twat, I thought.

"That bad, huh?"

I did a double-take, wondering if Jack had read my mind, because I know for certain I hadn't replied aloud.

Jack smiled charmingly as he played with the spare fork, rolling it between his fingers. "From what I can tell, I never really stood much chance of coming off well with someone like you though, did I?"

Our conversation was abruptly cut short, as the three waitresses had annoyingly made their way back to the table, one with her phone gripped tightly in her hands.

"Sorry to bother you," she blubbed, "but would you mind taking some photos with us?"

Jack plastered on the biggest, widest, smuggest smile I'd ever seen. "Yeah, of course!"

He took her phone and practically threw it at me. "You don't mind taking a photo of me with my fans do you, Mel?"

I ground my back teeth together and begrudgingly obliged. All the while thinking *I hate him. I actually hate him.*

Click. Click. Click. Photos taken. A flurry of thanks given — none to me, of course. And, before I knew it, Jack was draining his coffee and pulling on his coat.

"Right, I better be off," Jack headed for the door. "Try to remember me next time we meet, would ya?"

He then gave me his signature waft of the hand, and, with a jingle of the bell, he was gone.

I want to say I casually got on with my day after I lost sight of him. But that would be a lie. A big whopper of a lie. I literally did nothing else but fester and fume over that prick. His words circled around my head for the rest of the day.

'*I never really stood much chance of coming off well with someone like you though, did I?*'

Someone like me? What the hell had he meant by that? Was he calling me prejudiced? Or just accusing me of being unable to relate to someone like him? Because I'm normal and he's not. He's famous and I'm not. I'm just some run-of-the-mill Yorkshire lass with frizzy hair and wonky teeth, who in any other situation Jack Hart-throb wouldn't be seen dead with.

15th January

Why go through the stress of thinking someone is mean when it's so much easier and funnier to just assume that they're stupid?

I have to act opposite Jack today. It's just me and him all morning, until Jasmine joins us at lunch and I actually have someone decent to talk to. It's only one scene, I have to keep telling myself. And the quicker I get it done, the faster it will be over. I'm a professional, I can do this. And, as annoying as it is to admit, Jack is a good actor. He could be a prat *and* untalented. There's plenty of them out there. *Oh God, my pick-up is gonna be here in five minutes.* It's only one scene. It's only one scene.

Something is wrong. I was meant to be on set well over an hour ago. It's basically midday and nothing has been filmed from what I can tell. There's been no rearrangement of scenes, no cameras breaking, no plague hitting the entire crew (that I know of)... so what? I'm going to ask one of the runners. This is getting ridiculous.

Toby, the base runner, has unfortunately just been on the receiving end of a Director Andrew hissy fit because — *surprise surprise* — Mr Hart is the one holding up production. Jack's only gone and done a vanishing act. Was in his trailer ready to go one minute, and then *poof* — now no one can find him. I suggested to Toby that he look round the back of Studio B as Jack's probably trying to get off with a star-struck, gooey-eyed extra. *Apparently they've checked.*

It's been like a witch hunt. Everyone has been stumped and filming has officially been suspended. To put it nicely, it's unprofessional. To put it how I actually want to put it would require a lot more swearing. How can anyone — I don't care who the hell you think you are — how can anyone be so bloody selfish? I'm here because I want to work, not because I want to sit on my arse in a scratchy dress all day waiting for some second-rate bellend to get his act in gear.

Maybe Jack's that opposed to acting with me he's done a runner. Or maybe he rang his agent and refused to work until I'm fired and a fitter, more qualified, actress is placed opposite him. No, let's think more positively — maybe he's been hit by a bus.

Ugh. I need a drink.

What a bloody awful, pissing day.

16th January

Just choked on a blueberry. Chocolate wouldn't have done that to me. Just saying.

Because of yesterday's antics the entire schedule has been thrown right out of whack. I thought Jack might've been too embarrassed to show his face, but there he was sauntering into the breakfast tent. All eyes were on him, including mine.

I was sitting at a table with a couple of mates in the crew. Simon and Warren from the prop department, and Ose, a sound engineer. Conversation immediately turned to gossip about what had actually happened yesterday. Within seconds the rumours got laughably absurd. I didn't mind. It just assured me that my opinion of Jack was shared.

"I heard he found a grey hair," Simon mused. "Had a full on breakdown. Cried his eyes out."

"I heard it was food poisoning," Ose countered, devouring a spoonful of baked beans. "Shat his pants and costume didn't have any spare."

Everyone laughed but me. My eyes had landed on Jasmine and Jack in a tight embrace by the coffee machine. They did look good together, that was undeniable.

"You think he's found his next victim?" Simon pondered aloud. "She'd make his third co-star girlfriend this year."

"Think he's actually still dating the last one." Ose chipped in. "From that God-awful *Violins* show he's doing. Katherine Kay or something. Katlyn Kay? Kasey? It begins with a *kicking k* — Jesus, what's her fecking name?"

"Does anyone actually care, Ose?" Warren drained his coffee. "Right, sorry, Mel, love. We've got to be getting on with our work."

"Bout time," I teased.

Warren gave me an affectionate wink and off he disappeared. Simon, shoving the last of his butty into his mouth, followed close behind.

"Alone at last," Ose smirked.

I rolled my eyes, noticing Jack and Jasmine were now gone. *Weird*. Jasmine usually sits with me at breakfast and asks me to run her lines with her.

Ose picked up his breakfast box and slid closer to me. "So, how long have we got you for?"

"I'm not sure after yesterday, but the schedule says four more days."

"Is that it?"

I nodded.

"Looking forward to getting home?"

Definitely not.

According to Ian, he'd landed a new boyfriend. According to Amarra, Ian had acquired a squatter. Holding true to Ian's usual bad taste in men, his new 'boyfriend' is unemployed, on the drugs, and party mad. So home was no doubt going to resemble more of a bombsite than *Symbol of Freedom*'s literal bombsite set.

House-mate hell aside, I also didn't want to return to what currently felt like a different life. Here, life was good. Life was interesting. Back home my days are filled with; call from Dad, waitressing shift. Do a self tape. Call from Dad. Fixate over a job I haven't heard back from. Waitressing shift. Food shop. Call from Dad. Write in my diary about the nothingness that is life...

Now I'm in more of a low mood than I even thought possible. Face full of ice cream, curled up in my hotel room bed feeling sorry for myself. No, Jack didn't go missing again, but he *did* steal my friend. Jasmine barely spoke to me today. There was a brief "Hello", a definite "Goodbye" and a throw-away, "Where are you sitting for this scene? Just so I know where to direct my eyeline."

Jack said even fewer words to me. I think a 'Hi' was all he could muster. I wanted to bring up yesterday with him. Demand an apology for not only myself but the entire crew. But because Jasmine was being so friendly with him, it completely knocked my confidence. I felt like a third wheel in the worst possible way.

They were chatting. Giggling. Dare I say, *flirting*. It became evident within minutes why these two had been cast opposite each other. Palpable chemistry. Pissed me right off.

It all came to a sorry close when Jack invited Jasmine out for dinner. Claimed he was 'completely clueless with where was good in town', and would Jasmine be so kind as to take him somewhere for dinner? I was sitting right there. Jasmine agreed, and that was the end of that.

I got no invite. So here I am, alone. Knew it was all going too well.

17th January

Online journalism is the breeding ground for most evil. Well, that and my nana's knicker drawer.

My phone blew up this morning. We're talking atomic level, no survivors, just a big ol' nuke of mass destruction. Two pictures were to blame, surrounded by a load of 'news' that I didn't understand. The first was Jack and Jasmine, clearly from dinner last night, and adjacent to it, Jack and me. *Me!* Sat opposite Jack in that café. We definitely didn't look as cosy as Jack and Jasmine, but that didn't stop the caption from stating: 'Love Triangle seeming to form as Jasmine O'Connell and mystery woman are seen on separate secret dates with Jack Hart while filming their new hit for the big screen.'

    I didn't know what to think. I had missed calls from friends, an abundance of texts from family, and an insane amount of social media messages from people I hadn't spoken to for years. The one common factor of all this attention were the words, '*Is this you?*'

    I really wish it wasn't.
    My phone is ringing. It's Dad.
    Oh, hell.

"I just don't understand. Why didn't you tell me, Freckles?"

Dad's heartbroken voice sat heavy in my stomach. I felt sick. I was going to tell him eventually, it had never occurred to me he would, or even could, find out any other way about my new job. But apparently not. He can still access trashy online British magazines in France. Especially ones that have been sent to him by every mutual family member.

"Your Auntie Angela has sent it to me four times, Freckles. She's really upset that you didn't mention you had a new boyfriend."

"He's *not* my boyfriend, Dad." I looked at the photo again. "They must have taken this as soon as he sat down. We were only talking for like ten minutes and then he left for work." I scrolled down, rereading the article. "Bloody hell, I'm being accused of being the homewrecker of a six-month-long, fan-favourite relationship. *Jesus* — where have they got this from? It says here me and Jack have been seeing each other for a while. I only met him last week!"

"What's the saying? There's no such thing as bad publicity?"

"It is bad publicity when it's putting you up against one of your co-workers. There's a poll here for who Jack should continue pursuing. Me, Jasmine, or his ex, Kimberly Kay. Guess who's coming last?"

"Why do you care, Mel?" Dad queried. "Do you like this boy?"

"Absolutely not," I hissed. "He's an A-List knobhead. However, I *do* care about his fan base jumping on this psychotic bandwagon. It says here: '*Many Violins in Vienna fans are devastated by the news of Hart and Kay's rumoured split, some heading online to vent their outrage. One writing: 'Jasmine and his mystery woman have got nothing on our Kimberly, what on earth is Jack thinking?'. Others, however, like the new potential couples, one writing: 'This might do Violins some good! Jack and KK's on-screen chemistry was getting stale!'* Oh my God, it's bollocks, it's all just absolute bollocks!"

"Freckles, if you keep reading you're going to start spiralling."

Start? Couldn't he tell I was already down the rabbit hole and spinning on my head?

"Sorry, Dad, I just... This has never happened to me before."

"It comes with the new territory, I think," Dad mused.

I scrolled through the unread messages on my phone. Fifty per cent of them from Ian, losing his mind. Maybe not telling people had been a massive mistake.

Dad then sighed heavily, in a way that immediately told me he was gearing up to saying something that was about to make everything so much worse.

"I'm very proud of you, Melissa, and I know your mum would be too."

And there it is.

My brain was still in absolute tatters when I finally arrived at work. I'd decided it would be best to just leave my phone in my hotel room, and take a few hours away. Otherwise, I'd have just continued to scroll, and scroll and scroll. *No, thank you.*

Found Jasmine alone, sat in the green room, flicking through her scenes for the day. She looked up at me, a little flustered, and smiled. "Oh, hello."

"Hi."

I sat down beside her and a heavy, awkward silence fell over us. Suddenly, all I could think about was whether she'd seen the article too. Were she and Jack on a date last night and I'd awkwardly just got thrown into the mix? Should I bring it up? *God, I might have to.*

"How was dinner?"

"Good, I think. We went to that noodle place," Jasmine turned her script over. "Some photographers showed up, which wasn't great, but it happens. Did you have a good evening?"

"Oh, yeah," I lied. "Can't beat a tub of ice cream in bed by yourself."

"A tub?" Jasmine laughed. "You are joking, right? I assume you put the rest in the freezer."

I raised an eyebrow. "Does *your* hotel room have a freezer?"

She thought for a moment. "No, it doesn't."

I smiled. "Well, neither does mine."

Awkward silence again. *She mentioned photographers so maybe she wants me to bring up the article?*

"I don't suppose you've seen or been sent—?"

"Hello, ladies." At that moment, a tall man with round bifocals approached Jasmine from behind. His grey hair slicked back, his posture so upright he reminded me of a yard stick you'd find in an old school room. He placed a boney, wrinkled hand on Jasmine's shoulder, flashing a beaten up, gold wedding ring. Jasmine's demeanour almost immediately changed as his fingers seemed to bury themselves into her skin.

"Mr Elliot," she sprang to her feet. "I didn't know you were coming in today."

Mr Elliot? Was I supposed to know who this was? The name didn't send any bells ringing.

"Just to watch some of the rushes, Jasmine. And have a discussion with Andrew about this morning's rewrite."

"Which one?" I snorted. "We've had about six."

Mr Elliot's eyes landed on me. Piercing blue, full of a life no doubt wildly lived.

"The lemon amendments..."

"Jesus, I think production are running out of colours. But got to give it to them, they're getting imaginative. I've only ever had like blue, green, red, the usual draft names. But here, we got mauve yesterday. And then this morning they pulled out 'blush gold'," I rambled.

Jasmine was looking at me like a rabbit caught in the headlights. Her eyes were so wide I thought they might pop out of their sockets.

"Mel," she said with a slight warning underlying her tone. "This is Mr Charles Elliot, the Executive Producer, and owner of the production company."

Ah, balls.

"Mr Elliot, this is Mel, she's playing my sister."

"The comedic relief...?"

Was that a rhetorical question or a statement? I wondered.

"Melissa Bishop. I remember your audition tapes. Very bolshy."

Bolshy? My brain started to reel. Is that a compliment? An insult? Is it even a real word? I shook his hand, his skin unnaturally soft. *This man hasn't worked a day of manual labour in his life.* He didn't let go, just placed his other hand on top of those fingers already intertwined, and locked me in. "How does it feel being Jack's *mystery woman*?"

I felt my arse-hole clench, my stomach flip, and my cheeks flare up.

"I—"

Jasmine laughed, pulling both mine and Mr Elliot's attention. "Don't they come up with rubbish? Anything to sell a story, but at least they mentioned the film quite a lot."

Mr Elliot nodded, his hands still gripping mine. "You know what they say, there's no such thing as bad publicity."

I forced a very strained, very uncomfortable laugh. "Funny, that's what my dad said."

Mr Elliot finally let go, his eyes narrowing. I felt like he was scanning me, looking past my freckle-infested forehead and into the very depths of my skull. Sifting through my thoughts, and rummaging around in my insecurities. I felt my face grow redder and redder, sweat was starting to run down the back of my dress.

"*Charles!*" A familiar voice called. Jack swooped in, cutting between Mr Elliot and myself like a blunt pair of scissors. "I didn't know you were coming in. Good to see you!"

Jack's gone posh. *This is hilarious.*

Mr Elliot seemed to be lapping it up. Dear God, it was a match made in heaven.

"Surprise visit to catch a glimpse of the rushes, Jack. Andrew says you and Jasmine are exceeding expectations."

Both Jasmine and Jack smiled. *Am I the only one picking up on that backhanded compliment?*

"Jasmine is outshining us all," Jack beamed, taking Jasmine under his arm, practically forcing me out of the conversation all together.

The three proceeded to talk frivolously, continuously batting the compliment ball between each other. 'You're amazing.' 'No, *you're* amazing.' 'We wouldn't be able to be amazing if you hadn't been so awesomely amazing enough to allow us to be part of the project.'

Ugh. No offence to any of them but I'd rather lick my own arsehole than somebody else's.

"Are you okay, Mel?"

I suddenly realised Jack had hold of my arm. Jasmine and Mr Elliot were nowhere to be seen.

"Yeah, fine," I pulled my arm out of Jack's grasp. "Why?"

"Just Charles is a bit of a—"

Jasmine returned, bursting into the green room as though she had a mouse in the back of her dress. She wriggled and cringed, her fingers flexing. "Oh, God, he gives me the creeps."

Jack took three swift steps away from me.

"He asked me to have drinks with him before he flies back," Jasmine continued. "Not 'go out' for drinks. Oh, no. *Have* drinks with him in his hotel room. Saying something about *more unnecessary* publicity for the film as an excuse. Oh, and Jack, he also recommended *we* don't go for dinner again, by the way. What a joke."

I felt Jack's eyes flicker my way. *Crap.* Had he seen the article too? Oh God, what if he thought I was a leak? What if he thought I was so madly in love with him I'd fabricated an entire relationship in my head and leaked it to the press? No. He probably doesn't think that... I hope.

"It's a shame Mr Elliot barely spoke to me," I mused, trying to break some of the tension.

"Shame? Be grateful, Mel," Jasmine shuddered. "*Very* grateful."

"Hard to be when we're encouraged by our agents to schmooze with the likes of an executive producer. Networking, I think it's called?"

Jack frowned, his eyebrows drawing together. "Networking is a load of bullshit. Made up by people like Charles to get naive actors like you to wander blindly into their hotel rooms."

"I'm not naive," I stammered.

Jack rolled his eyes. "Yeah, okay."

I felt my cheeks grow hot, but then spotted Jasmine nodding in agreement out of the corner of my eye.

"We all learn the hard way, Mel. Find ourselves back at a director's house thinking if I drink this drink, laugh at his jokes, snort this key, let him kiss my neck or whatever then he'll cast me in the lead for his next massive project." She laughed heartily, not processing how serious and unfunny everything she was saying was. "But it's always the same. They're too drunk, too coked up or horny to even remember their own name, let alone mine when it comes to casting."

Jack laughed along with her and I almost felt like they were having me on. Was this just common knowledge? Was this the standard practice? Or just all some sick joke?

"I've even had it," Jack added. "Execs, producers, directors, whoever, trying to make a pass at me. Usually some part dangled in front of me like a carrot on a piece of string. You learn to navigate around it. Stopped auditioning for this one theatre where the artistic director uses the top floor for his shenanigans."

"I know the one you mean," Jasmine added cheerily.

"Jack, that's not normal..." I trailed off.

"See? Naive," Jack chuckled, pointing at my slightly agape mouth. "Unfortunately, Mel, it *is* the norm."

"And that makes it okay, does it?"

Jasmine flicked through her script aimlessly. "It's not like we can do anything to change it. Not if we want to keep working."

I put my head in my hands before scrubbing my face, frustrated. "I'm sorry, I thought the industry had improved? I thought we'd moved on from casting couch scenarios? And sleazy men smoking cigars, who buy young actors' bodies with false promises of Hollywood?"

Jasmine tutted. "You're taking this too seriously, Mel."

I don't think you're taking this seriously enough, I thought, my heart rate quickening.

"It's improved, sure," she continued, "especially on the scale you're talking about. It's more...*subtle* now. You've got to keep your wits about you and not put yourself in any situation that could be misinterpreted. You have to keep yourself safe. No one else will."

I couldn't believe it. A woman who claims to be a feminist, shouts to the high heavens about equal pay, and is the face of the 'true feminine rage' frontier, talking like this? 'Not put yourself in any situation that could be misinterpreted. *You have to keep yourself safe*'. That almost sounds like victim blaming — Hell, it *is* victim blaming.

Jasmine then changed the subject. She completely shrugged off the gravitas of what she'd just said and started chatting about something else. Suddenly we were hearing about a new bath bomb she'd just tried.

A sour taste filled my mouth.

If this is what it means to be a successful actor in the industry, then I don't want to be one.

18th January

Told Mum once I was thinking of getting a dove tattoo on the side of my right boob. Her response? 'Give it twenty years and that dove is going to be a fat pigeon.' I took note.

I never thought I'd say this but I'm ready for *Symbol of Freedom* to be over. Not only has another article, with my actual name on it, been printed, but more photos of Jack and I together. I don't know how, but some photographer has managed to capture photos of Jack and I leaving our separate trailers and merged them together.

I looked horrendous beside him. To a point where it made me feel sick just looking at it. The article purposely made the image of us together look farcical. The finger pointed at me, encouraging the reader, as if saying to them, "Go on, look at her. Doesn't she look stupid? Doesn't she look ridiculous? Isn't the idea of her dating Jack the most hilarious, stupid, depressing thing you've ever heard?'

The addition of my name has meant a tsunami of random people have flooded my socials. Comments from strangers at the bottom of old photographs have made me incredibly aware of my own body, in a way I didn't even think possible. They all discuss in length the copious amount of freckles I have, my 'not so subtle' double chin, and my poor posture. Jesus, one bloke even decided to comment how he thought my boobs *'Look like crushed cloves of garlic under that top'.* I've concluded this man has never seen a pair of tits in real life and is just pissing his opinion into the wind.

I thought I'd be stronger than to let any of this get to me, but now I find myself staring at my photographs, listing all of my external and internal faults. *It's becoming a bloody long list.*

There was a heavy knock on my trailer door.

"Come in."

Toby poked his head in. "Sorry to bother you, Mel." As he spoke, his eyes swiftly scanned the room. "Don't suppose you've seen Jack anywhere have you?"

Other than the million times I've looked over his face when triple checking these articles? I thought.

"No, I haven't. Why?"

Toby looked sheepish. "He may have gone walk-about again."

I jumped up onto my feet and threw my phone into my bag. "You've got to be joking. Where was he seen last?"

"Heading to set about an hour ago, but he still hasn't shown up. We've managed to swap scenes to keep Jasmine occupied but if we don't get him on set in the next hour it's not going to be pretty."

Toby let me past and I scanned the base car park. Lines of trailers scattered about, like a white, rusty, metal maze. Where do you even start? *It's like trying to find a twat in a haystack.*

"Right."

I took off in a random direction.

"Where are you going?!" Toby called after me. "I can't lose you too!"

"I'll be right back," I encouraged with a throwaway thumbs up. "If Jack wants to play hide and seek, Tobes, game on."

If it weren't for the smell of smoke I never would have found him. Jack was sitting round the back of some prop lorry with his feet dangling over the edge of the opened up trailer. I approached with caution, hearing him speak quietly on the phone.

"I told you, I can't come see you at the moment. But in a couple of weeks, I'm all yours."

Another woman? That would make four of us.

"Do you think you'll be able to hold on for a few weeks?" Jack went quiet, and all of a sudden his feet went very still. "Can I call you back? Yeah, you too."

A sickly feeling began to bubble in my stomach, and the hairs on the back of my neck began to stand up on end. I knew instantly I shouldn't have been there. I took a few steps back, all the while thinking, *Well I've found him. I've done my bit. Production can take it from here.*

"I know you're there."

I froze.

Jack sat up and looked me up and down.

"You know it's rude to listen in on people's private conversations."

I couldn't help but pull a face. He may have had a point but—

"It's also rude to not show up to set when there's an entire cast and crew waiting for you, mate."

Jack's left eyebrow raised. He almost looked shocked I'd spoken to him with a little bit of venom in my tone.

"I was just—" He bit the inside of his cheek. "That was a serious phone call I needed to take. Not that it's any of your business."

"It is my business when it stops me from doing my job," I hit back. "I'm just trying to prevent a repeat of the other day."

"The other day? You talk awfully confident for someone who has no idea what they're on about, Mel." Jack jumped out of the back of the trailer. Infuriatingly, I found myself almost gawking. I was unprepared to see him in full fighter pilot get-up, and my God, the uniform was doing him a few favours.

"I had to leave *the other day* for an emergency. A *private* emergency," Jack brushed himself off before glaring at me expectantly. "Well?"

"Well what?" I blinked.

"Well, let's get a move on since you're *so* bloody desperate to get me on set!"

My jaw clenched.

"It's not about you, Jack. I couldn't give a crap about you. It's about all the other people here who have a job to do, myself included. Who don't fancy spending another day twiddling their thumbs waiting for you to finish *umming* and *ahhing* about whether or not you're going to show up for work. You may have an *emergency* going on but communication is key if you don't want to piss off a whole production team."

Jack took a moment. It looked like he was contemplating shouting at me but then he looked down at his phone mournfully instead. He scrubbed his brow with the back of his hand.

"I'm being a knobhead aren't I?"

I snorted. "Just a tad."

"God, what a nightmare," he groaned.

There was something about the tone of his voice that made all the anger in my body evaporate. It struck a chord in a part of me that I try to avoid. That sad, sorry, grieving part of me that still thinks about my mum.

"Want to talk about it?" I asked, without really registering what I was saying. Of course Jack wouldn't want to talk about his problems. Especially with me. He probably has a six-thousand-pound-an-hour therapist to talk to about it. God, why did I ask?

"It's my grandad," Jack trailed off. "He's umm—"

"How long has he been given?"

Jack went rigid. His broad shoulders tense, his eyes staring directly at me, baffled. "How'd you—?"

I shrugged. "Call it a hunch."

Jack let out a half-exhausted laugh. "Good hunch. I'm impressed."

"Don't be. I'm speaking from experience."

Before Jack could ask, I raised my hand. A universal sign for, *don't even get me started.* Now was not the time or place to go into the whole dead mum back story.

"They say he's got a couple of months. Could be a year, if he's lucky." Jack shoved his phone into his pocket, and ran his fingers through his hair. "I'm not dealing with it all that well, if you hadn't noticed."

"I'd say, considering the situation, you're doing a hell of a lot better than most people would."

Jack half smiled, exhausted. "Thanks."

We stood in silence for a good minute before I could no longer help myself.

"Not to sound too insensitive, but I think we better head back now."

Jack nodded, all the fight I'd seen moments ago drained out of him. He matched his stride with mine as we headed back towards base.

"Sorry about the other day."

Did he just say sorry?

Jack mumbled, no doubt apologising didn't come naturally to him. "It was the day my grandad got his terminal prognosis. Production was supposed to be shut down but there was a miscommunication somewhere. I don't really know what happened but apparently no one got told to go home. Must've been awful."

"Yeah," I agreed. "I even contemplated giving that *Violins* a watch, I was so bored."

Jack faked a laugh. "Did you?"

"Oh, God, no," I teased, "I said I was bored, not desperate."

I couldn't tell if he was faking a laugh again or genuinely finding me funny. Most probably the former. I was insulting the shining star of his life's work, after all.

"Tried to do some writing instead, but wasn't very successful, so I just scrolled on my phone."

I trailed off. Having mentioned my phone, my mind had decided to throw up a million of the hateful comments I'd read. I crossed my arms over my stomach, wondering if Jack was aware of the new articles. Had he seen the comments beneath them and thought the same things his fans thought about me?

"What are you writing?" Jack asked, pulling me back into the present.

"I'm not *really* writing." I began to feel myself panic. Why did I say I tried to do some writing? I literally opened up my laptop, stared at a half-arsed play that I've had writer's block with for God knows how long, and then gave up. "It's just this silly little script. It's nothing really."

"That's cool," he feigned interest. "What's it about?"

"Err... A woman who is at a crossroads. She spends most of the play contemplating what to do next."

Hearing myself say it out loud made me realise how silly and little my play actually was.

"Sounds interesting, I'd love to give it a read sometime. When it's finished."

Yeah, right, I joked inside my head. *Never gonna happen.*

19th January

Apparently I'm supposed to ignore the police tape outside of reception. It's proving difficult.

What to do? WHAT DO I DO? Production have only gone and shoved the scene I have with Jack on the end of today's schedule. If it wasn't already chock-a-block enough. So not what I need right now. This morning has been filled with Jack being annoyingly charming. Like, he's been warm and attentive, and I have no idea why. I told Amarra on the phone this morning that I don't trust it.

"It's like Jack has a nice switch that he's just miraculously decided to turn on," I ranted. "I feel like maybe he knew he was on the road to losing his job or something so now he's overcompensating. I mean, like, get this — yesterday he went on set and *apologised* to everyone for his lateness. The whole crew, even Jasmine, who didn't even know he was missing. He said as a way of apologising he'd get pizza, and I kid you not, fifty pizza boxes showed up. It didn't even phase him."

"The guy must have cash to burn," Amarra grunted. "Have you been back on your socials since that second article about the two of you came out?"

Oh, God, my socials. I'd taken the easy way out and just turned them all to private. I was slowly but surely working my way through the hate. Deleting every nasty comment, blocking every troll account, and completely ghosting Ian until I got home.

It sounds silly, but actually taking control of what I can, in a situation that I very much can't, has helped. Sort of.

There was a knock on my trailer door just after breakfast and my heart sank a little. I was preemptively thinking it would be Toby again, Jack having done a proper runner this time. Not because his grandfather was dying, just that he had finally come to his senses and didn't want to act opposite me.

It wasn't Toby.

It was the man himself. Jack. Nervous and clumsy. Almost falling into the trailer having misjudged the step coming up.

"Sorry to bother you," he stuttered. "Just wondered if you would be free for a line run? Jasmine said you're quite good at them."

Jasmine and Jack talk about me? I thought, a touch panic-stricken. "Yeah, sure."

I put down my diary. Jack's eyes followed the goofy, sticker-infested notepad.

"Sorry, were you writing? Have I interrupted? I can just wait till we're on set."

"Give over," I laughed nervously, clearing some space on the small sofa. "Do you want to sit, or—?"

"No, I'll stand." Jack shuffled from one foot to the other. "I wasn't really expecting this scene to come up today. I thought they'd bang it on the end of the shoot or something. But apparently that would mean bringing you back in May, and they'd rather just get it done while you're over here. When do you go back?"

"They've got me on the 6am flight, the day after tomorrow."

"Oh, so you're pretty much done then?"

"Pretty much," I nodded, feeling an odd tension fill the tiny trailer. Or maybe I was just imagining it? I lifted my sides after an awkward moment of silence. "Shall we...?"

"Are you looking forward to going back?"

Funny how that always seems to be the follow up question.

"I don't know," I shrugged. "I've loved being here but it's had its ups and downs. Hotel life can only go on so long without driving you crazy. I'd appreciate doing a load of washing, and being in my own bed, to be honest. But I'm going to miss working."

Jack's eyebrows pulled together. "I thought you said you had a couple of opportunities lined up? Have they all fallen through?"

I bit my tongue. That's the thing about casual lying, you have to have a good memory in order to be any bloody good at it. "'Fraid so," I replied, thinking it would be better to just drop the act, than try and fool this guy into thinking I had anything more than a waitressing opportunity waiting at home for me.

"I'm sorry to hear that."

Is he? I wondered. *Or is he just saying that because it's the decent thing to say?*

"Anyway, you came here to run lines, not talk about my career." I looked down at the script and cleared my throat. "So, do you want to run the whole thing or just your lines?"

"The whole thing, preferably," Jack wiped his hands on the back of his jeans. "Thank you for this, by the way. I really appreciate it. And thank you as well, for yesterday."

I looked up at him and something in me did a little summersault. He sounded quite sweet, even genuine. It was almost touching. "You're welcome, Jack."

"But I do have a favour to ask."

"Including the one I'm already doing?" I joked.

Jack didn't laugh. "Would you mind not telling anyone about yesterday?"

The somersaulting stopped, immediately, and my heart rate began to quicken.

"I don't know if you've seen, but there's been a couple of things written about us over the past few days. Some really repulsive stuff has come up because of it."

Repulsive? Jack thinks the idea of him and I dating is... repulsive?

"Now, I know you know they're just making stuff up, but just be careful. Because if there is a leak, or a source, whatever you want to call it — I just want to make it clear that I don't want anyone knowing about my grandad's condition."

My blood began to boil as I realised one of my biggest anxieties was actually true. Jack really did think I was the *'insider source'*. He believed I was telling the press about us. Making things up. Fabricating an entire relationship. Madly in love with him, and trying to convince the world he was in love with me, when really he thought the idea of dating me *repulsive*.

"Jack, I would never—"

"I'm not saying that you would."

"I think that's exactly what you're saying," I snapped.

Jack's lips went thin and his cheeks became flushed. "Mel, I'm just telling you to keep what I told you yesterday to yourself."

I shook my head, trying to calm myself down before I kicked him out. I had to remain professional despite internally raging. I really thought, really believed this prick could be nice. But I couldn't have been more wrong! Because here he was accusing me of being a fantasising lunatic of a snitch, who he would never date because he finds the idea of dating me, and therefore me as a person… *repulsive.*

On set Andrew, surprisingly, noticed something was off with me. It took him an hour but I'll give him credit, he was actually looking at me today. He crept out from behind his monitor and approached me. Jack was pacing in front of me, mumbling his lines under his breath.

"Would *you* mind trying a take that's a little softer?" Andrew asked me. "Try not to glare at Jack so much, it's coming across very intense."

Jack's ears pricked up at the mere mention of his name. "Anything I can do, Andrew?"

Kiss ass, I thought, rubbing my temples.

"I think maybe a little more attention to her. Really focus all your lines this way rather than throwing them out to the room. Think tunnel vision."

Some directors aren't half full of shit.

We went for another take, and try as I might to soften my face, I was still called out for glaring at Jack. I couldn't help it, the word 'repulsive' was playing on repeat in my head.

Jack leaned into me, while Andrew discussed some lighting issue with the gaffer.

"Are we okay?" Jack asked, dumbly. "You've been acting weird since this morning."

"I'm fine," I lied. "Just want to get this scene done. It's going on forever."

Jack pulled a face. "Okay."

There was an uncomfortable pause. Crew scuttling around us, a light being changed, a lens being flipped. "Do you want to go for dinner, after we wrap tonight?" Jack suddenly asked.

It completely threw me off guard. I blinked at him dumbly. "What?"

"Just as it's your last day tomorrow. We don't have to," he laughed nervously. "Just an idea…"

I was so tempted to ask, 'Are you sure? Aren't we not supposed to? Don't you have any worries that we might be pictured together? Or that I might leak our conversations to some journalist? Won't it be too repulsive for you?' But I didn't. We still had three more set-ups to do, and a last day of filming with Jasmine tomorrow. So, unfortunately I had to stay as professional as possible, which unusually for me, was proving quite difficult.

"Sure," I stupidly accepted. "Why not?"

11:56pm
I don't know why I'm writing the time. I feel it's because I need to. I need to write the time and the fact I've got three double rum and Cokes swimming round my system because that will provide the perfect context as to why I've just kissed Jack.

20th January

Dad always said, 'Bad experiences make life interesting'. I'm tired of an interesting life. I'd like a dull one from now on, please.

My head hurts.

I feel like if I get up from my bed I will collapse onto the floor and not have the strength to get back up again. And believe it or not, it's not because I'm hungover. I'm not. I'm just dying of embarrassment. Internally shrivelling up at the horrific fact I threw myself at the world's fourth sexiest man last night.

We'd wrapped late, both exhausted, but for some reason, Jack was adamant he was going to take me out for dinner. So we went, and I started drinking. *Oh, God.*

The restaurant was nice. The staff were pissed off that we showed up half an hour before closing, but all was quickly forgiven when Jack gave an outrageously large tip upfront. I thought I'd go for something small to get dinner over with as quickly as possible, but then Jack went ahead and ordered four separate starters, three mains, and almost every side available on the menu.

"You've got to be taking the piss," I said to him, just as the waitress scurried off with the longest order for two people ever.

"What?" Jack shrugged, sipping his pint. "I'm hungry."

"It's bad enough we walked in just as they were wiping down the kitchen, but now you've gone and ordered half the menu. Couldn't we have just got a drink, and let them go home?"

"Why do you care?"

I bit my tongue, genuinely a bit embarrassed to admit I work the majority of the time in the hospitality industry. I've been that poor waitress, who's probably been here since God-knows-when, whose feet hurt, and all she wants is her bed.

"We're the only ones here," I pointed across the deserted restaurant, "I just feel bad for the staff, that's all."

"It's their job." Jack folded his arms across his chest. "And I'm paying them aren't I?"

I took a hefty gulp of my double rum and Coke. "God, you're so obnoxious." Another gulp, "I just think you should be a little bit more considerate of people's feelings Jack, okay?"

Jack's left eyebrow raised. "Are we still talking about the staff?"

Another gulp and another and another, and another. The bubbles burned my throat, the rum warming my chest, filling me with liquid courage. "You just sometimes say things without giving much thought to the possible consequences. Like, you say things that are hurtful, but you don't really seem to care."

"Oh, and you don't?" Jack snorted. "You made me feel about *this big*," he pinched his thumb and forefinger together, "after you spat out that entire speech about how ridiculous drama schools are. And even smaller when you mocked me for going to one. Making yourself out to be better than me because you never went to drama school."

I wiped my mouth dry with the back of my hand, my glass drained. "I never said I didn't go to drama school."

Jack paused, thrown. "Well, did you...?"

"Sort of."

Jack scowled. "It's not a sort-of question, Mel. You either did, or you didn't."

"Technically, I did, yes. For the first month, and then I dropped out."

"...*Why?*"

Unable to stop it, the sound of my mum crying down the phone suddenly filled my ears. I could suddenly see myself curled into a ball on my bedroom floor, Freddie awkwardly standing over me, unable to comfort me, my mum explaining that her days were now numbered.

I swallowed hard, casting the painful memory aside.

"It just wasn't for me."

I avoided any further questions by flagging down the waitress and ordering another double rum and Coke. Then once she'd gone, I swiftly changed the subject.

"So, how does your girlfriend feel about you being away for so long?"

Of all the things to come out of my mouth, that was the last thing I expected to actually make it to the front of the line.

Jack smirked against the rim of his still very full pint glass. "I don't have a girlfriend," he confessed, though I already sort of knew that. I think.

"Oh, I'm sure I read somewhere that you were dating that," I racked my brain for one of the names Ose had said. "Katie? Kayleen? Something or other."

"Kimberly?"

I began to play with my empty glass, suddenly very aware of my hands. *Where's the food? What's taking so long?*

"Yeah, Kimberly isn't my girlfriend."

"You broke up then?"

Jack shook his head, "Not as such. We weren't ever really together."

I felt my eyes roll. "*Oh really?*"

Jack pushed the basket of complimentary bread across to my side of the table. "Yes, really. We went on like one date during the first season, quickly realised it's stupid to dip your pen in the company ink, especially with two more seasons being commissioned. And called it quits. Though the fans responded so well to the possibility of us dating that the show owners orchestrated a PR stunt."

"A PR stunt?" I snorted, shoving a piece of bread in my mouth.

"You never heard of one before?"

"In movies!" I said, breadcrumbs spraying about. "And, like, gossip columns. But they're not real!"

Jack gave me a look, his previous comment about me being *'naive'* coming to the forefront of my mind.

My jaw dropped. "As if?"

Jack simply nodded, and sipped his pint again. Maybe he had a point, maybe I am naive. So completely clueless about an industry I thought I knew quite well. But then again, this is a level of the industry I've never been at, and probably never will be a part of.

"How's your play coming along?" Jack asked, just as the starters, and my second drink, were brought to the table.

"Not great," I confessed. "Writer's block is a biatch, as usual."

"What are you struggling with?"

"Literally, what to write," I snorted, amused by my own incompetence. "I haven't a clue what I'm doing."

"Have you tried writing what you know?"

"Meaning what?"

"Well, that's the saying, isn't it? Write what you know. So, this woman being at a crossroads, deciding what to do next, is that something you've experienced? Have you been through what she's going through?"

He remembered the summary I gave him?

"Sort of. I mean, at the moment I'm writing that she's stuck between the boyfriend she's with, who is a bit of a bellend — not nasty, just not right for her — and the bloke who she likes but who's also in a relationship, and emotionally unavailable."

"Right. And you've been through that have you?" Jack smirked, clearly finding the idea of me being in the middle of a love triangle almost laughable.

"You find that hard to believe?" I asked, my face burning up. I gulped down some more of my drink, growing more infuriated by Jack's lack of response with every second of silence that ticked by. "There are some blokes out there who don't find me *repulsive,* you know."

Jack's eyebrows furrowed. "Why would you even say that? No one thinks you're repulsive, Mel."

"You do."

I drained my glass, Jack's face having turned to stone. He blinked at me, completely thrown. Probably taken aback by the fact I'd even had the balls to call him out on his crappy behaviour.

"Like I said before," I continued, "Sometimes you say things without thinking, and those things can be really hurtful. Like this morning, you said that the articles about us were repulsive. That the idea of us dating is repulsive. That I am repulsive."

There was a long pause before Jack broke out into a deep, joyous laugh. "God, I knew something had got your knickers in a twist today but bloody hell, that is mental."

"It's not funny, Jack."

Jack sipped his pint, still chuckling under his breath. "Oh, but it is. You literally heard me say, 'some really repulsive stuff has come up' because of those articles, and you make it about you."

"You weren't talking about me?" I asked, dumbfounded.

Jack shook his head. "I've had messages from Kimberly's psychotic fanbase accusing me of breaking her heart and making her suicidal, for well over a week now. I've had newspapers call me 'a womanising, misogynistic player'. When, in reality, I was taking Jasmine out to try and get to know her a little better before I snog her face off for the next four months."

I blinked. There was so much to unpack. So much I needed to apologise for. However, one thing Jack said had taken precedence. I couldn't let it slide.

"Did you seriously just say *snog*?" I laughed. "Who the hell says snog nowadays?"

Jack rolled his eyes and slid one of the starter plates towards me. "Shut up and eat some food, you mad bint."

We continued to eat and drink — actually beginning to enjoy each other's company, dare I say. As the waitress cleared our table, Jack asked, "What do you plan on doing with the script when it's done?"

I stared at him blankly. *I can't even get my act in gear to get it finished, let alone think and plan about what to do with it after.*

"I have a couple of contacts I can give you if you want to get it on the fringe scene. Or, I can always ask my agent if he knows of any literary agents who are scouting?"

"I don't need your pity, Jack," I snapped. I wasn't sure why he was being nice to me but I was getting an iffy feeling about it. Or maybe that was the four shots of rum sitting in my stomach.

"I'm not giving you pity," Jack rubbed his brow, frustrated. "It's called networking."

"Which you said was bullshit."

Jack pondered, "I did say that, yes."

"So, if it's not networking, and it's not pity, why are you being nice to me?"

"Because I like you."

What? He liked me? I felt like I was going to burst into flames, my face had grown so hot.

"Do you want another double rum and Coke before I pay up?" I think I heard him ask.

Another drink? I'm going to need one.

Jack had said he liked me. Like, those actual words. No ifs. No buts. No coconuts. Just plain and simple. Jack, the blonde, Hollywood heart-throb had just said he liked me. *Holy crap.*

Jack paid and in the freezing cold, my head still spinning, we made our way to the hotel. The rum coursing around my body convinced me I was warm enough but Jack wasn't having it. He was adamant he could see me shivering, and gave me his coat. Despite the lingering smell of smoke, the leather was warm and comforting. Jack lit up a cigarette, and offered me a drag.

"You don't smoke?"

"No. I have tried though," I replied, purposefully omitting the fact I tried once when I was thirteen behind the back of the bike sheds at school. I got niccy rush so bad I threw up on my friend Mariam, who then spent the rest of the day in a PE kit our teacher had dragged out of lost and found. Mariam hadn't known which was worse — smelling of my vomit, or someone else's cheesy veruca BO.

"How much do I owe you for my half of the bill?"

Jack shook his head, "Nah, tonight was on me. We were supposed to be celebrating your last day being tomorrow after all. You can get the next one."

Next one? I swallowed the hard lump in my throat. *I really wished at this point that I hadn't downed that third drink.*

We passed through a completely deserted reception, and as we stepped into the lift I felt a sudden shiver run down my spine. I was being torn by two very stubborn and furious parts of my brain.

One half was telling me this was the guy who had willfully ignored me on multiple occasions, mocked my naivety, and been obnoxious and egotistical, and I knew I really despised him.

But then there was the half of me that was screaming out that this guy *liked me*. He'd made a point of telling me he didn't have a girlfriend, and he had paid for dinner, so was this in fact the end of a date?

What do I usually do at the end of a date? I don't even know. I can't actually recall the last time I went on a date. *Jesus, when was the last time I kissed someone?* It wouldn't have been Freddie so that would mean the last person I kissed was —

Suddenly I was wondering what it would be like to kiss Jack. Would his lips be warm? Soft? Would he taste of smoke? Or beer? Would he put his hands on my waist? In my hair? Wrap his fingers round the back of my neck and pull my body close to his?

That was the moment I then threw myself on him.

I don't know what came over me but before I knew it I was on him. And then I wasn't. Just out of the lift and running to my hotel room, which just seemed to be getting further and further away. I fell into the room, and slid to the floor, my head in my hands.

What. A. Dickhead.

I've managed to avoid Jack all day. It wasn't too difficult as it was clear he was also trying to avoid me. I could say I wanted to apologise to him for what happened. But that would mean speaking to him, and with this being my last day there was really no point.

Jasmine came to my trailer with a bunch of flowers, a nice surprise, and gave me a big squeeze. She only had a few minutes to express her gratitude for all the line runs and 'girl chats' and hoped we'd work together again soon, though that statement came out with very little conviction. We both knew deep down how the industry worked, and how very unlikely it was that we would see each other again.

I headed out of my trailer and towards Dermot's car where he was waiting for me. It had been almost a month of him driving me to and from base and I still couldn't understand a single word he said.

He opened up the back passenger door. "You got everything you need, Mel?" I heard him ask. But he could have been telling me I 'had an interesting smell'. *God knows.*

As I was about to clamber in, Jack yelled, "Oi!" from the other end of the car park. He started jogging over, still in his pilot uniform. I felt like there should've been an orchestra playing somewhere to really complete the leading man aesthetic he was going for. "Thought you could sneak away without saying goodbye?"

That was the plan, I thought.

Jack made his way around the car and wrapped his arms around my waist. "Come on, then. Give us a squeeze."

I reluctantly hugged him back. Then it occurred to me this was perhaps a perfect moment to apologise.

"Look about last night—"

"Don't worry about it," Jack shrugged, pulling away. "It was... *cute.*"

Cute? No guy who is interested in a girl refers to her drunkenly mauling him as *cute*. Clearly, when he'd said 'I like you', he meant only in a platonic way. I needed to backtrack — save myself any further embarrassment and turn the conversation around so I didn't come across as a desperate loser.

"Yeah," I stepped away from him, "I was just going to ask you what happened. I don't really remember anything past leaving the restaurant."

"Oh," Jack's eyes widened, "Well... nothing really. I just walked you back to your hotel room and then we — well you... you went in, and I went to my room."

I'm glad he went along with it. Maybe he does have a half-decent bone in his body.

"Was nice meeting you, Jack." I said, without thinking, passing him the bunch of flowers Jasmine had given me. "Good luck with everything. And your grandad, I hope it all goes well with him."

I then fell into the back of the car, and immediately cringed into the back seat.

Why had I said that? Why had I ended my brief existence in Jack's life like that? Of course all isn't going to go well with his grandad. The poor bastard is dying. He's a ticking time bomb for Jack, and I— *Oh God.*

I'd become one of those people who I hated while Mum was sick. They'd say things like, 'At least she's in a better place', or, 'At least she's no longer in pain', or my absolute favourite, 'Everything happens for a reason'.
There's no right thing to say to someone who is in the midst of losing a loved one, but there are a hell of a lot of wrong things to say, and I'd just spat out a top contender.

I'm going to be overthinking that horrendous goodbye for the rest of my life. I swear, I'll be on my deathbed, thinking back on that moment and weeping. Or maybe I won't? Maybe it wasn't that bad...

... It was that bad. I'm never going to get over this.

21st January

Jet lag from a 30-minute flight is unlikely, but not impossible. Kind of like getting an STD at a Christian Summer Camp — it happens.

Ian hasn't left me alone since I walked through the front door. I'm tired, hungry, and coming down from a three-week-long adrenalin high. He hit me with a machine gun of questions before I'd even set my bags down.

Who did you meet? Who did you talk to? Who were you friends with? Who *this*. Who *that*.
The lad has turned into a pissing owl.

24th January

It's Mille-Feuille. Pronounced, Mill Foyer. Not milly filly. Not Miller Furr. And certainly not, 'Ere, love, I want a vanilla slice.'

Well, I can't say I'm surprised but I've not been home for three days and I'm already back waitressing. It's not like I was expecting to come home to the bells and whistles of a million job offers lined up, but I was hoping for *something*. An email from Bethany just saying 'Hi' would've been enough. Instead I got a text from Charlie asking if I could cover their shift. So now I'm putting cake and skinny cappuccinos down in front of people, trying to convince myself this last month did actually happen.

Only a few days ago I was having lunch with Jasmine, going through outfit choices for her next red-carpet appearance and flicking through images of shoes that cost three times as much as my rent. Now I'm mopping piss off of a bathroom floor.

I was scrubbing down the toastie maker when I got a slight tug on my apron strings. It was Oliver, reaching over the counter, grinning smugly.

"You look well fit in that," he said, pulling me in for a kiss on the cheek.

It threw me. Oliver hadn't so much as shook my hand before (not including the ass rubbing at *Carlo's),* let alone given me a kiss.

"Glad to see you're back from Hollywood in one piece." He propped himself up against a table and crossed his extremely large, tattooed arms across his chest.

I laughed nervously. "Yeah, only got back a couple of days ago."

"Tilly said."

I wondered how Tilly knew my filming schedule? But without even asking aloud Oliver said, "She met up with Ian last night."

That answered that.

"Ian also said you've been rubbing elbows with the bitch and famous?"

I rolled my eyes. Mr Blabbermouth had struck again.

"He's just chatting the usual rubbish. Ignore him. Anyway, before I get the sack, what can I get for you?"

Oliver puffed out his chest slightly, scanning the menu hanging above my head, grinning mischievously. "I'll take a coffee, and a date, if you're not too famous."

"Righty ho."

What a moment to use that phrase for the first time.

The problem with organising a date so spontaneously is no time, place or activity is actually decided on. All Oliver had said was, "See you at yours tonight, then."

That's it. Is 4pm too early to be night? 5pm? Oh, God. Did I even want a date? Was I ready for a date? It was only five days ago I was locking lips with... *Yes, I need a date,* I told myself sternly. I need to well and truly let what occurred during *Symbol of Freedom* go. Zone back into my *actual* life again, and partake in anything that makes it interesting. Including going on a date with Oliver — whenever he decides to show up.

It's 7pm. I've changed outfits three times. My hair four times. And tried to eat and talked myself out of it six times. I'm sat here like a lemon. I've no idea where we're going or what we're doing. I'm currently dressed and ready for a dinner date; my hair is up, wearing nice heels, nice dress, etc. But five minutes ago I was dressed for an activity date. Like bowling or mini golf, so wearing jeans and trainers.

My head is mush. This is officially going to go down as the worst date in history, if it does even happen. I'm ringing Amarra to get her to do some damage control, talk me off the edge.

"Why don't you just text him?" she asked me down the phone. "It's not unreasonable to just pop him a message saying, 'Just a quickie, what time were you thinking and what's the dress code?'"

"What if he's changed his mind?" I replied, pacing the length of the living room. "What if he's not coming at all? Imagine I message him that and he's not even on his way."

"Then he's a bigger bellend than even I thought he was capable of being."

At that point there was a heavy knock on the door.

"I'll call you back."

I swung open the front door. Waiting on the step was Oliver. Gorgeous, sexy Oliver, wearing jeans, a nice shirt and... *Is he seriously holding a bottle of wine*?

"Hello, Hollywood," he kissed my cheek then stepped over the threshold, letting himself in.

It wasn't a date.

It was a hook-up.

To be honest, I'll take what I can get.

8th February

I have lost all confidence in how to spell the word February. The first 'r' is throwing me right off.

This month could not be going any slower.

Ian is obviously bored with me. After weeks of giving the same answers of:

"Sorry Ian, Jasmine was lovely. She wasn't a bitch. There was no drama."

"Ian, I don't know if Jack is back with his ex-girlfriend."

"Don't ask me anything about Andrew, he didn't even bother to learn my name."

Ian is now nowhere to be seen.

The house is instantly untidy after I clean it, and I can hear snores coming from under his bedroom door, so I know he's not dead. Just not interested in me and my no-longer-showbiz life.

Oliver has also dropped off the radar, unsurprisingly. Our hook-up had gone as well as they ever can go. There's some awkward chat, a not-so-comfy cuddle on the sofa while watching a film. Then without warning and out of nowhere - *hey ho* - a boner. A miniscule amount of foreplay. A semi-decent shag. A wipe up and a kiss on the cheek goodbye.

Not exactly the stuff of rom-coms. Not that they're realistic at all anyway. The couple always have sex and then cuddle. *How?* No one ever questions the lack of birth control in movies, because when you do, it makes you realise how stupid they all are. If there was a condom, it would be removed almost instantly.

If there wasn't a condom then there is no way she is lying there wasting time. She's in a race against gravity. If films were realistic, she'd be up like a shot and hobbling to the toilet. Hand cupped under her fanny, praying that nothing plops out and stains the carpet.

Amarra calls it a 'cum run'.

16th February

Life is about patience and trust; of which, I have neither.

Yes! FINALLY an audition! It's a really good audition too, a supporting lead in a new comedy film. The premise sounds fun, if a little tacky. Regardless, I'm thrilled and I'm grateful.

The more I read the script, the more I'm convinced I could really get this. With *Symbol of Freedom* now officially under my belt, I'm bound to at least get a callback. It's not like I lack the credentials: I've been in a film before, I've done comedy before. If this industry worked the same way as all the 'normal' ones, I would say I'm fully qualified. I could land this.

Finally, something I can focus on that isn't a black forest gateau order, or an electricity bill. Winner, winner, chicken dinner.

18th February

The lyric I've had stuck in my head is something along the lines of, 'There ain't no rest for the wicked' — I think that applies greatly to the acting industry. The horrible actors, with the worst reputations, always seem to be the ones forever in work.

Tilly was being weird. It's not like her to call me up out of the blue, for no reason at all, and ask to go for a coffee. I thought maybe she'd finally found out about Oliver and me bumpin' uglies, and wanted to put me in my place. But no, she literally got me out of my pyjamas, away from the safety and comfort of my duvet, and into a snobbish, overpriced, artisan coffee shop to talk about work.

"I don't want a big song and dance like we had for *you*. So, I'm telling everyone who needs to know one-on-one…" She took a big, dramatic pause. "I got a job."

"Oh, yeah?" I humoured her. "What's the job?"

Her eyes sparkled with pure delight. "It's a lead in a new streaming series. Ten episodes. I fly to Jamaica on Friday."

I almost dropped my brew.

It only took me a few seconds to pull myself together. Tilly clearly wanted a big, jealous reaction out of me, but I wasn't playing that game. I wasn't going to give her the satisfaction of knowing she'd got to me.

"That's brilliant!" I forced a smile and reached across the table to give her hand a squeeze. "Oh, I'm so happy for you," I lied.

Any actor who says they're happy for their actor friends when they land roles is lying. That's why actors are rarely friends with each other. You can't be happy for someone who potentially took a job that could have been yours. The only reason Tilly and I have lasted this long is because our casting types are polar opposites. She can't do comedy, or anything that requires a northern accent. And I can't do whatever the hell it is she's good at. *I'm yet to find out what that actually is.*

Tilly let out a sigh of relief. "Oh, thank God. I almost didn't tell you. What with it all going quiet on the job front since you got back. I didn't want it to come across like I was rubbing it in."

Of course you didn't, I thought. *For someone who's taken more acting classes than anyone else I know, Tilly really is awful.*

"I mean, I'm assuming it's still quiet," she pushed. "Is it? Or has Bethany been able to scrape an audition out of the bottom of the barrel for you?"

"Well, now that you mention it, yeah, she has. I've actually got an audition tomorrow afternoon. Another movie, so a great follow on from *Symbol*. I've met the casting director before, and it's a comedy part, so it should be a good one."

Tilly's eyes widened ever so slightly. "Oh, that's great..." she trailed off, no doubt calculating her next move. "I'll see if any of my mates have gone up for it as well — keep you in the round robin for when it gets cast so you know not to keep your hopes up unnecessarily."

I couldn't help but suck my teeth. It might have been because I was already in a foul mood, but Tilly was coming across bitchier than usual. *Maybe it's because she knows you've bounced on top of her brother,* I considered. *Maybe this is her way of getting back at you.* No, if Tilly knew Oliver and I had hooked up, she wouldn't even be speaking to me.

Now there's a thought.

"Forgot to ask, how's your brother doing?"

"He's fine. *Why?*" Tilly's eyebrows furrowed, her face turning from smug to suspicious.

"No reason," I smiled wickedly. "Just, I have one of his socks. Found it under my bed the other day when I was doing the hoovering. Wondered if he might want it back."

3rd May

Pale blue is such a lovely colour. Just a shame I can't wear it to any occasion ever. I sweat too much. I'm a sweater, if nothing else. And pale blue is such an unforgiving colour when it comes to sweat marks.

It's been weeks since my audition and I've heard nothing. It's excruciating. I really thought I nailed my meeting too. I made the casting director laugh. I'd impressed them with all my anecdotes about my time on *Symbol*. None of which included the moments where I'd thoroughly made an idiot of myself, of course.

I just need somebody to put me out of my misery. The whole 'no news is good news' line is wearing thin. According to the email, they don't start filming till 14th May, so there's still hope. They could be still weighing up their options. I could still be in the running.

Mum suggested, when I first started out as an actor, that I should buy myself a bunch of flowers whenever I go for an audition, and then if they're dead before I've heard back, I know I haven't got the job. Was a nice idea, till I had a graveyard of flowers in the kitchen, and was found sobbing in a pool of my own tears on the floor, adamant there was still hope.

'Don't throw those away! I know it's been three months but they could still call! It could be any day now — don't throw them away!'

My phone is ringing. *Oh, God, it's Bethany...*

Infuriatingly, Bethany didn't mention the audition at all. She was too busy nattering away about this bloody *Symbol of Freedom* wrap party. I'd received the email invite a week ago and just assumed it had been sent to me by mistake.

"Personally, I think it's a great opportunity, Mel." *Agent translation: you need to go.* "It's a private event in a bar just opposite Soho Theatre. There shouldn't be any press, but there will be all the execs, some of the cast, crew, et cetera." She took a deep intake of breath. "And as I said, it's a *really* great opportunity."

Agent translation: you have to go, *or else.*

Before I knew it I was standing, hair piss-wet through, in my dressing gown, looking at my haggard reflection, wondering why on God's green earth I'd said yes. A wrap party, for Pete's sake? For what purpose?

I facetimed Amarra, thinking she would be able to provide some form of comfort. She didn't. I'd perched her on my windowsill so she could get a full view of the hot mess she was dealing with. Outfit after outfit being rejected. Too casual, too formal, too summery, too wintery.

"What are you doing with your hair? Having it up or down?"

"Why does that matter?"

"Well, if you have your hair up, and like some dangly earrings, it'll make your jeans look less casual. Especially if you put it with a sexy top."

"I don't own any sexy tops, Amarra."

"Well what about a skirt then?"

"I haven't shaved my legs."

"You could wear tights."

"They've all got ladders in them."

This is what we deal with, every single time we have to make an outfit decision. A wardrobe full of clothes, and yet nothing to wear.

"What about your nice denim jacket?" Amarra sipped her wine and pointed off-camera. "The one hanging on the back of your door."

I pulled on my jacket and we both hummed. *Denim on denim? Absolutely not*, we no doubt thought in unison. I ripped the jacket back off.

"Have you got any nice dresses?"

I foraged through my dresser and extracted the poor excuse of a dress Ian had given me for Christmas. "I have this?" I joked, but Amarra wasn't laughing. She was snapping her fingers and dancing across my phone screen, wine raised high in the air.

"Yes! Oh my God, yes!"

I rolled my eyes. "Over my dead body."

She pushed her face as close to the camera as possible. "Mel, please. I'm begging you. Shave your legs in the sink, get your face done, get your hair up, whack on some hoops and rock that dress."

"It's a flannel, Amarra."

"It's genius."

How had Amarra convinced me to do this? My body was wrapped in a sliver of green fabric, my legs covered in cuts from a rusty razor, and my hair in a frizzy ponytail doused in hair spray. The tube was full of people in sweatpants and jeans. I felt obscenely overdressed. A few eyes looked my way and I felt myself riddled with insecurity. It threw up all those comments people had made about me when those articles came out all those weeks ago. '*Her tits look like crushed cloves of garlic under that top*'. I shuddered. Maybe I should have worn a push-up bra. Maybe I should *own* a push-up bra.

Reflecting on those comments made me think about the one thing my brain had been trying to avoid from the moment the invite had come through.

Jack. God, I felt sick.

I'd convinced myself he wouldn't be there. He'd already be on to the next job. No time for silly little wrap parties, attended by silly little people, like me, who are available at a moment's notice because they have no active social life/life in general.

My brain had thrown up every worst-case scenario on the walk from Leicester Square tube station to the venue.

My biggest fear? I would arrive and have no one remember me, because why would they? I wrapped four bloody months ago.

I felt like drinking my worries away but felt fearful that it would somehow end up with me finding a picture of myself online tomorrow, blacked out on the pavement, using a slice of pizza as a pillow. Little did I know that would have been preferable compared to what was actually in store for me.

Security let me in, one not so subtly scanning me up and down as I squeezed past him and into the venue. It was a poorly lit bar littered with burgundy leather booths. *Cringe.* The place was packed — filled to the brim with tonnes of people I didn't recognise. No Warren, Simon, Toby, or Ose — *no one under the age of forty...* That realisation was enough to make me turn and bolt.

Only I'd not paid close enough attention to my surroundings and instead of finding myself back at the entrance, I was suddenly outside in a smoking area. Three people, huddled around a fire pit, surrounded by a haze of smoke.

These three I *did* recognise. Not from filming, but from online. *Oscar Izir,* beauty guru/model. *Eleanor Stanski,* supermodel. And *Kimberly Kay,* actor and Jack's ex PR stunt girlfriend.

"You alright, Boo?" Kimberly looked up from the flames. "You look a bit lost."

"Well—" I choked, feeling a little like a lamb chop that had just been thrown into a glamorous, botox-filled hyena den. "I was looking for the toilet," I improvised, "must've taken a wrong turn."

"I can show you, love, hold on." Kimberly stubbed out her cigarette with her glittery heel. "Follow me."

As she took my arm, I got a strong wave of perfume. Eye-wateringly strong, like when you walk through the glass doors at a department store and it takes four floors for the smell to dissipate.

"I swear I recognise your face," she whispered, just as the door slammed shut behind us. "Were you at Stanski's show last Friday night?"

No, I thought. *I was in my local corner shop buying German meatballs and a bunch of scratch cards last Friday night.*

"Don't think so," I laughed nervously, mentally acknowledging the fact she probably knew me from the articles that claimed I'd stolen her fake boyfriend.

Maybe it's no longer fake? I thought. It then occurred to me that Kimberly had no real reason to be here other than as Jack's plus-one. And if Jack's plus-one was here, then so was the man himself.

We entered the fluorescently-lit toilets and I rushed into the nearest cubicle, hoping and praying Kimberly would now leave, so I could make a proper escape. "You must've been desperate," Kimberly called from the other side of the door. "Are you not with anyone?"

I dabbed my forehead and pits with some toilet roll. "No, I'm on my own."

"Oh." I heard a tap running. "Well, you should come hang with us. We're just waiting for Jack to come back."

I could've smashed my head against the toilet bowl. Why had I said I was on my own? Why was God, or my guardian angel, or whoever is in charge of my life, doing this to me? *Sick bastard, whoever you are.*

"He went out for some more ciggies. Do you smoke?"

I reappeared from the toilet and found Kimberly perched next to the sink, fixing the tiny pink strap of her top.

"No, no I don't," I said quietly, hoping that didn't make me uncool as it so often seems to with people who do smoke. I washed my hands with Kimberly watching me, idly swinging her legs back and forth.

"I don't either. Not really. I social smoke, you know? Can't do an acting job these days without smoking. If you don't smoke you miss out on all the good gossip."

I nodded, even though I hadn't the faintest idea what she was talking about. The mention of 'an acting job' must have connected a couple of dots in her brain though because Kimberly's face suddenly fell.

"Are you an actor?" she asked, hopping down from the counter. "Were you in this?"

"Yeah," I confessed. "Only a small part though."

"Oh!" Kimberly's face lit up, "You'll know Jack then. Amazing! He'll be so relieved to see someone he actually worked with. We've had nothing but office people from production he's never met because Jasmine's on some shoot in Toronto, and so many of the crew are Manchester-based and couldn't make it down." Kimberly took my arm again after I dried my hands. "Why they didn't just throw the wrap party up there is beyond me. Would've loved a cheeky city break in Manchester! Like have you been to Canal Street? It's ace — Not like this dive!"

She pulled me out of the toilet and back the way we came. I felt like digging my heels into the beer-stained carpet. I was hating every second of this. There was no way of convincing Kimberly that Jack would almost certainly not be relieved to see me. Especially if all hasn't gone well with his grandad since we last spoke... *Oh, God.*

The fire door to the smoking area clunked open and Kimberly skipped out, her heels clicking against the concrete. In any other situation I'm sure we could've been great girl besties. 'Girl besties' in the sense of you meet a girl at a party, who's usually pissed as hell, in the bathroom and within minutes you're in platonic love. You hype up each other's outfits. Over-share your life within minutes of knowing each other. Build up each other's confidence higher than anyone else in your life has before, only to leave the bathroom never to see or think about each other ever again. That kind of girl bestie.

Jack had his back to the door and was hunched over the fire pit, engulfed by smoke. Kimberly patted him on the shoulder, and as he turned I felt my knees almost give way.

"God, you look sexy," was the first and only thing to come out of his mouth.

I could've dropped dead.

As if he just said that. *As if he just said that in front of all of these people.*

"Doesn't she just?" Kimberly beamed, either genuinely unphased, or just that good of an actress she was covering it well. "That dress is stunning."

"Charity shop, four pound fifty," I answered without thinking. Northern habit; someone compliments you on your outfit and you automatically tell them where you got it and how much it was.

In normal circumstances, you're usually met with, 'ooo's and, 'aahh's, especially if it was a bargain. But around company that probably never live in the realms of single pounds and pence, I was instead met with four blank faces.

I smiled awkwardly. This was the universe giving me a clear cue to leave before I embarrassed myself any further. Jack took a long drag of his lit cigarette, breaking out into a grin that stretched from ear to ear.

"Kim, Oscar, Eleanor, this is Mel."

Oscar and Eleanor beamed, and Kimberly, if possible, got even more friendly. "Mel?" she smacked Jack's shoulder. "Why didn't you say sooner! We've heard so much about you!"

Oh, good God.

"All good things, I hope," I laughed nervously.

Jack took another drag. "Can I get you a drink? Double rum and Coke, yeah?"

My jaw clenched and despite attempting to bite my tongue, the words "Just water this time" came tumbling out of my mouth.

For the next two hours I tried my best to make every excuse to leave, but nothing could shake them. Oscar was eager to know everything about my time on the job, keen to get every detail of what Jack was really like to work with. With Jack present, I only spoke of the good stuff, complimenting his natural instinct, while still joking that "Even if his acting in the film is crap, no one is going to care while he's wearing that pilot uniform".

As soon as Jack mentioned I was an aspiring writer Eleanor was babbling about her favourite books and plays.

Kimberly wanted to know why I got into acting. I gave a vague answer, bits and pieces of the truth muddled together with the generic, "It's just always what I've wanted to do." I continued, "I was really lucky to have supportive parents."

"Wish my folks were like that," Kimberly mused. "My dad especially is dead set against what I do for a living. He says my acting career is basically just prostitution by another name."

"Can you blame him?" Oscar teased. "The poor bloke has had to see you get your kit off and simulate sex in almost every role you've played."

We all laughed. Really laughed. Except for Jack, who was just quietly observing from the corner, staring at me. It made me wonder what I was doing wrong.

"I think I'm going to head home," I blurted out.

"Already?" Kimberly queried. "We were about to hit a couple of clubs, you're welcome to join us."

"Yeah, sorry," I stalled. "It's just that I've got an early start tomorrow."

"Do you want me to order you a cab?" Eleanor got out her phone but I protested.

"No, it's fine, I'll get the tube."

Jack drained his pint then stubbed out his cig. "I'll walk you."

Kimberly did a double-take. "Jack, there's like twenty photographers scheduled to be outside. Let Oscar walk her, or Eleanor."

Jack rolled his eyes. "We'll go out via the back," he kissed her cheek affectionately. "I'll be careful, Kim. See you in ten."

I wish Jack hadn't offered.

I wish I hadn't agreed.

We managed to sneak out of a back entrance and after a quick jump over a series of bin bags we were on the main road. No photographers in sight, though I smelled like a rotten banana.

"Which line do you need to get?" Jack asked, trying to start a conversation.

"Piccadilly," I replied, purposefully not giving him much to work with. The less conversation we had, the less chance there would be of me saying something stupid again.

"You had a good night?" Jack tried again.

"Yeah, your friends are nice."

"They're not really my friends, to be honest, they're Kimberly's mates. She brought them because I didn't know how much schmoozing I'd need to do, and she didn't want to be on her own all night."

"*Schmoozing?* Isn't that just a fancy word for networking?" I snorted disdainfully. God, this man is a walking contradiction. "Remember? *Networking* — that bullshit that's only for naive actors like me."

"I mean, schmooze as in say thanks to all the folk who helped to make the film. Not kiss their asses and beg for an innings when the next casting call comes rolling out."

"Fair enough," I shrugged, not fully convinced. We walked a little more. Eventually curiosity and genuine interest got the better of me. "How's your grandad doing?"

Jack's face fell a little, but then he softly sighed and forced a grin. "He's doing good. Responding well to his treatment. Struggling on his feet but still able to live independently so that's something."

"That's great," I encouraged, my heart undeniably going out to him. "And how're you feeling about it all?"

Jack shrugged and we left it there.

I wasn't going to push it, especially with the station entrance now in sight. The time had come to say goodbye, and this time I wouldn't jump him or say something stupid and insensitive. I'd play it cool, and leave him with a positive, everlasting impression of me. After all, he had called me 'sexy'. *Yes, good plan, Mel.*

"Well, this is me," I pointed at Leicester Square's bright, shining, dark blue sign before rummaging around in my purse for my card. "I've just got to find my—"

A pair of lips suddenly landed on mine; warm and smooth. The stubble on Jack's upper lip tickled my skin. His hand caressed the curve of my waist and I felt as though I was melting into his touch. *I'm going to turn into a puddle.*

The kiss felt like an infinite moment. Time suspended while my brain tried to catch up with the reality that Jack was kissing me. His lips were on me, *voluntarily*. The kiss lasted longer than it should have done, but also nowhere near long enough.

He pulled away and I was left, legs shaking, feet frozen to the spot.

"Was good seeing you, Mel."

"Yeah..." I trailed off watching him turn on his heel and walk away. "Good seeing you, too."

7th May

Is it still a booty call even if I have no arse?

Work was a shambles. I almost dropped my tray five times. Couldn't get my head on straight, my brain going over every detail of what occurred at the wrap party, trying to figure it all out.

"Are you alright?" Charlie asked as I half stumbled into the cake display. "You've been an airhead all shift." They let a gasp of steam out of the coffee machine.

"Yeah, fine. Just—" I clenched and relaxed my fists three times over. I knew the reasons why I was a mess, but I wasn't prepared to admit to it.

God, you look sexy.

I spilled the new delivery of sweetener sachets all over the counter top. "For God's sake!"

Charlie wriggled their eyebrows knowingly at me, the milk they were frothing bubbling over. "Looks like you're in need of a de-stress. Go get yourself some, take your mind off it."

Their head fell back with laughter as I shot them a sharp look.

"I don't need a shag, Charlie. I need a job."

"You are aware you're *at work*, right?"

"An *acting* job," I hissed, knowing full well they were winding me up on purpose. "I need my agent to ring me up and tell me, 'You know that part you went up for a month ago? Yeah, well, the lass they did cast broke her ankle and can't do it, so the part's yours. Hooray!'"

"And what's the likelihood of that happening?"

"Not a chance in hell."

Charlie slid a perfectly poured latte towards me. "So, de-stress it is then."

Oliver's profile picture looked as posed as I remembered. Muscles flexed, tattoos pristine, sweatpants tugged down just enough to see—

Hey Ollie, you about? I've got a bottle of wine I need help with, M x

Pressing send had activated a pressure cooker effect in my stomach. I didn't even have a bottle of wine but I couldn't exactly write 'a bottle of sunflower oil'.

Bzzzt.

Oh yeah? ;) I can help with that! O x

Oliver was stood, smirking, on my front doorstep within thirty minutes, between my thighs within thirty five. Then breathless and finished within.... *Thirty eight.*

"I'm glad you hit me up, you know?" Oliver panted, wiping sweat off his brow with the back of his hand. "I'd actually just been thinking about you."

Liar.

"Oh, yeah? Cool."

"Yeah," he smirked. "A mate forwarded that article of you and Jack Hart to me the other day,"

Why the hell was Oliver bringing up Jack? I needed Oliver to be a distraction, not shine a light on the very thing I was trying to forget.

"And anyway, my mate was like, 'Don't you know her?' It was so cool. I was able to be like, 'Yeah, I do. I know someone famous, you know?"

"Does your sister not count?" I scoffed. "She's off in Jamaica filming her big series after all."

Oliver gave me a look. "Do me a favour. She's more likely to be kidnapped than get famous on the job she's on. Literally, she's in a place with a hostage warning on it. The job also sounds well dumb, no one's going to watch it."

Out of everything that had come from our hook-up, that was embarrassingly the only thing that put a smile on my face.

Oliver picked the dirt out from under his nails. "Don't suppose you have Jasmine O'Connell's number do you?"

My smile vanished. I sat up, reaching for my shirt. "I'm going for a shower."

God, you look sexy — For God's sake!

14th May

If God exists, I'd like to talk to him about his twisted sense of humour.

I've written off today as a 'fugdone' day, as my mum used to call them. Stands for, 'Fooking done with today and it's not even 9am'. It means you wrap yourself in a quilt cocoon, with hair and teeth unbrushed, and feel sorry for yourself.

It's official, I didn't get the movie I'd been holding out for. Filming started today, and obviously I'm not there. So, that's the end of that. I don't usually let the rejection get to me, but this was a part I really wanted. It was the next job that made sense. *Not that anything in this industry makes sense.* I get why casting don't let the 'unsuccessful' know they've not been picked, it would be so time consuming, but that doesn't make me like how it is. It's unfair — like living in limbo, never knowing how long this employment drought will last.

My phone rang loudly from the sofa. I shuffled across the cold, hardwood floor, clinging to my duvet, and answered.

"Mel?"

Oh my God. "Jack?"

"Yeah. Hi, are you free? As in *now* kind of free? I need help." His voice sounded strained, tense. God it was good to hear his voice.

"What kind of help?" A million different scenarios played in my head. Majority of them involved Jack tied up. The rest Jack tied up and shirtless. *Get a grip woman,* I thought. *You're turning feral.*

"I need help with an audition tape."

Disappointing.

Jack breathed deeply. "I've just got back from LA and I need it done in like the next couple of hours. No one else is around so I was wondering if you were free to read with me?"

"Err, yeah? Sure."

"Have you got space to film?"

"Are you wanting to come here?" I looked around the living room and through the door into the kitchen. It was a mess, from floor to ceiling.

"Would that be okay?"

I hesitated, and if Jack had sounded any less desperate I would have said no. But he *did* sound desperate.

I finally caved and gave him my address.

"Oh, cool. Well I'm just coming out of Heathrow Airport now. So I'll jump in a taxi and be there as soon as I can, then hopefully Michael will get off my ass."

Jack hung up.

That was it. I felt like ringing back and telling his arrogant arse not to bother but he'd withheld his number. I breathed deeply. I didn't have time to rage. Jack was coming over... from Heathrow? What did that give me — an hour, maybe? Sixty minutes to get myself and this house looking semi-respectable. That meant getting my knickers off the radiator and these toast crumbs out of my cleavage.

The knock on the front door was never going to come at a good time. I felt sick to my stomach and was nowhere near ready. I'd fantasised about Jack a lot this month, it had been hell. 'God, you look sexy,' was almost becoming my bedtime mantra. That kiss... That mind-boggling, completely out of character, sodding kiss had confused me to no end. I could get mad at him, really mad and demand answers about why he'd done what he'd done, but no. That wasn't going to help either of us. So, instead I'd decided I was going to be civil. A former co-worker who was helping out with a self tape. Not some bit of fancy Jack had kissed, and whose words, 'God, you look sexy,' had been my daily torment. Civil and nice, that was the plan.

I opened the door and was immediately met with, "I've got two hours."

Fuck the plan.

"Oh hi, Jack, good to see you too. I'm fine, thanks for asking. Yes, it has been a while. No, I've not been up to much. God, you're a prick!"

I slammed the front door shut. After a long beat, my heart thundering in my ears, there was a gentle knock. I opened the door slowly. Jack was smiling, holding back a laugh.

"Hi, Mel. It's been a while, how have you been?"

I rolled my eyes at him and opened the door fully. "You're still a prick."

He stepped over the threshold then wrapped me in a hug and squeezed me so hard I thought my breath would leave my body. After pulling away he kissed my cheek and whispered, "It's good to see you."

My whole body shivered.

After we finished filming Jack collapsed onto the sofa, and ran his fingers through his hair. It had grown a lot since I'd last seen him. The longer length suited him, made him look more relaxed. It also made his face brighter, and his eyes greener, somehow.

We'd made little conversation before filming his self tapes. Jack was too eager to get them done to make small talk. He really meant it when he said he only had two hours. And they were almost up.

"I genuinely didn't think I was going to get those tapes done, you know? Thank you for helping me out. You're a lifesaver."

"Anytime." I sat awkwardly opposite him, still unable to comprehend how I was keeping my shit together.

Jack was in my house.

"You think you'll get the job?"

"It's a weird one," he placed his hands behind his head, his shirt riding up. "They kind of already offered me the job, but they want me to tape for it as well, as there's some American executive who's not convinced I'm right for it."

I rested my head against the back of the chair and just observed Jack talking. A fortnight ago I'd accepted I would never see this man again except for on my TV, and yet here he was, as real as ever. His V-line peeking out from under the hem of his shirt and the smallest trail of strawberry-blonde hair, leading up to his belly button and down to his—

"Anyway..." Jack's eyes scanned the room. I hadn't had time to thoroughly clean, so I was sure he'd find something to comment on. "How are you?"

My breath hitched. "I'm fine."

"Working?"

"Yeah, I have today off, but back in tomorrow for eight hours. Though I know it's more likely going to be around twelve."

"Jesus, you need to have a word with your first AD if you're overrunning by four hours, Mel."

I couldn't help but laugh, Jack was naturally confused.

"I'm waitressing, Jack."

How different our lives were. Work to him immediately meant an acting gig.

"Oh," Jack's eyebrows furrowed and he frowned apologetically.

"Don't give me that look," I warned him. "I don't need your sympathy."

"Are you still auditioning?"

"Yeah, sort of. I had one about a month ago but didn't get it."

"You don't seem too bothered."

Now that's poor observation and a half, I thought. "I am bothered, Jack. Gutted to be honest," I signed heavily. "But this is the norm for me. Getting quite sick of it to be honest. Do you ever get tired of waiting for the next job? Thinking you could be doing something better with your life, rather than just sitting around going over every single detail of your audition, wondering what you did wrong? Or better yet, fixating on your last self tape, which took you hours to film, knowing casting are looking at the first five seconds and either giving a shit about you or not?"

"Great conversation considering I've just taped in front of you, Mel."

"Sorry, I didn't mean—" I scrunched my nose at him playfully. "What I'm getting at is, some of us don't have jobs just thrown at us."

I'd hit a nerve, and part of me wondered if I'd meant to.

"I don't get jobs thrown at me. Especially not ones I actually want. Don't go thinking I don't work hard, Mel. Because I do."

"I know you do. I've just witnessed it."

Jack's shirt was still lifted and exposing the muscle definition in his abs. I wondered what his skin felt like, what it'd be like to actually trace that light trail of hair with my finger tip... *God, I think I'm staring*. I swiftly looked away. *Did Jack notice?*

Jack watched me with a smirk. *Yes*, I answered myself. *He had noticed.*

"Talking of work, has the tape transferred through? Our WiFi can be patchy."

Jack patted himself down searching for his phone. He eventually found it buried between the cushions having fallen out of his back pocket. He retrieved a lace-trimmed piece of paper along with it.

"Think this is yours," he went to pass it over the coffee table but I wafted the damn invitation away.

"Shove it back where you found it."

Jack's curiosity got the better of him, his eyes darting back and forth across the glittery gold text. "A wedding invite?"

"Yeah, my cousin's. Her sole purpose in life is to convince me that I am inferior to her in every way, mainly because I'm single."

"You never took me as the jealous type, Mel."

"I'm not jealous. Believe me, Gareth is a drip with this weird squeaky voice." I rubbed my face just thinking about having to spend three days with my family. I could barely even make it through Christmas dinner. "My whole family is going to be there and they're just not... *normal*."

"No one has a normal family."

"Compared to mine, everyone has some kind of normality reinstated. Dad, bless his heart, is radged with no filter. I've got grandparents so polar opposite you wonder how in the hell they ever got together. I've got uncles with drinking problems, aunts with botox addictions, and a cousin who's had countless affairs with married men now turned blushing virgin bride-to-be. Give me a break," I sighed.

Jack shrugged, amused. "Again, no one has a normal family." He placed the invite gingerly on the coffee table. "I haven't been in a room with my entire family probably ever. No one speaks. My dad is a mechanic who left when I was six. Mum is God-knows-where, shagging God-knows-who. My grandad, as I've already told you, has a lot of health issues. And my brother? Well, he's been selling my stuff online. We're talking clothes, kitchenware, bedding, and if he could get his hands on some, I've no doubt he'd have a crack at flogging my hair from the shower drain."

I spit out a laugh.

"You're kidding?"

Jack shook his head slowly. "I've had six of his accounts suspended since Christmas."

"Jesus. You win."

"He wasn't always like that, just... Money changes people. And it's always the people you least expect who stab you in the back when you start to climb and become someone on the '*celebrity*' ladder."

I found myself chewing the inside of my cheek. I'd never considered the fact Jack might have anything other than a perfect family who all supported and loved him. How could he not, with a career like his? Maybe they were what I feared my family would become if I made it big — *indifferent.*

"I don't think anyone can boast of having a normal family. What even is *normal*?" Jack frowned, deep in thought. "Whatever they are, at least your cousin cares enough to invite you to the happiest day of their lives. In France, of all places."

"Ah yes, to walk amongst the fields of Provence on a spectacular holiday, completely alone but constantly reminded I could have brought someone." I rolled my eyes and tapped the 'plus-one' with disdain. "She's done it to spite me, you know? Willow knows I'd never bring any potential boyfriend to endure the kind of hell they'd throw his way."

"Then take a friend who likes a good laugh, and loves French wine. Who'll happily pretend to be your boyfriend, and put up with any kind of crap they throw for the sake of a few days' holiday."

I laughed heartily. "You sound like you're volunteering, Jack."

"And what if I am?"

I rolled my eyes. "*You* want to come with *me*?" Sarcasm soaked every word.

"Yeah, okay."

He lay back on the sofa and started to scroll on his phone, clearing his throat. "I haven't got anything booked that week and it's more than enough notice. I'm sure Michael will let me take a few days off. What's the dress code?" He wiped his forehead with the back of his hand, then ruffled his hair, pulling on the strands. "I don't want to pack a suit and then be surrounded by Hawaiian shirts, you know what I mean?" He stared at me expectantly.

My throat had gone dry and my palms had suddenly started to sweat.

"I don't know..." *Was this still a joke?* I wondered. He was taking it a bit far.

"Well, what are you wearing? Do you want to match and look all loved-up, or play it more believable?"

I shook my head. "Okay, hardy-ha-ha. Enough now, Jack."

Jack seemingly ignored me, continuing to scroll on his phone. "Do you want to fly down a few days before and we can make a whole week of it?"

"Jack..."

"I mean have you already bought your ticket? Because I have some spare air miles if you want a freebie—"

"Jack!" I snapped. My ears were hot and my heart was beating so hard I could feel it in my temples. "Would you just stop, okay? This isn't funny anymore."

His eyes went wide. "What isn't?" He put his phone away slowly. "Sorry, that was insensitive wasn't it?"

"You think?" the sarcastic tone rolled off my tongue. "I mean, I know it's been a while since we've spoken, but you kind of have to put the time and effort in before you start making jokes like that."

"Wait. Jokes like what? I know throwing a free ticket around could be a tad inconsiderate but I don't know what else I've done wrong here. What joke am I supposedly making?"

My heart landed heavily in my stomach, bile creeping up my throat.

He was being serious.

"You actually want to come with me?"

Jack blinked, bewildered. "Yeah..."

"*Why*?"

He laughed warmly, crossing his arms over his chest and relaxing into the sofa. "Because you asked me to."

20th May

Struggling to breathe this morning. Pray I'm not coming down with another sinus infection — if my ear gets blocked again, I'll sue.

It's been a week since Jack decided to pop into my life again. Part of me is still convinced I slipped on my duvet, hit my head and hallucinated the entire thing. But then, random texts have started to appear on my phone. When I say 'random', I mean *random.* Yesterday, I got the text: 'Milkshakes with ice cream in them, definitely superior, J'. And this morning — *even more random* — I got: 'Does anybody actually say 'ey'up chuck' anymore? Think it's just me. #sadtimes. J'.

If it weren't for the 'J' sign-off, I would've sworn Ian had used my number to sign up for some dodgy website and just not told me. Madness. This boy is pure and utter *madness.*

Amongst Jack's bizarre texts, I also got an email from Bethany yesterday. There were none of her usual niceties, just a brief, time, place, breakdown, audition scenes attached. She even signed it 'B', with no kiss. *Weird.*

I dragged myself to the audition this morning without having really done much preparation for it. Because every time I tried to knuckle down with it, I thought,

What's the point? It's an audition for a two-line part in a show I'd never heard of, and I knew deep down that it didn't matter. I wasn't going to get it anyway.

They were running a *tad* late. I rolled my eyes. I've gone to great lengths to be punctual, why can't they? I've had to find cover at work, I've washed and straightened my hair, I've waded my way through central London rush-hour tube chaos, and they can't even be arsed to see me on time?

Eventually they called me in, the casting director's assistant not even making eye contact with me.

"Megan, is it?"

"Melissa," I corrected. "Melissa Bishop."

"Right." She pointed at the space in front of her little camera. "If you could just say your name, age, height, and agent for me."

Please and thank you go a long way, Denise.

I straightened up and recited my info, "My name is Melissa Bishop, I'm five foot five, and I'm signed with Bethany Rollins and co."

"You forgot your age."

I smiled grimly. We both knew she wasn't technically allowed to ask for my age.

"I'm over eighteen," I stated bluntly, before lifting up my pages. "Now, which line do you want to start with?"

8th June

I've packed ten pairs of knickers for five days. You know, in case I shit myself... multiple times.

Ian paced the back of the living room. Amarra, hungover on the windowsill, sipped a steaming cup of coffee and I chewed away what little nail I had left on my right hand.

"Thought you said he was coming for seven?" Ian fretted.

"I did."

Amarra groaned. Any time of day that wasn't in the double digits didn't sit well with her.

"Well, it's five past seven and he's not here, Mel."

"I know he's not here, Ian," I chuntered, before pushing my suitcase out from under my legs. "Maybe he's changed his mind, or a job came up, or an audition, or—"

Amarra pointed through the curtains as she sipped her coffee drowsily. "Well, a car's coming up the drive," she yawned. "Pretty fancy one, too."

I've never seen Ian move so fast. He vaulted over the sofa and practically fell against the front door just as there was a loud knock. Ian swung it open, beaming. *Jesus, has Ian had his teeth whitened specially?*

"Jack!" Ian thrust a hand forward. I began to cringe, embarrassed on Ian's behalf. "Ian Klark. Nice to finally meet you. Heard so much about you."

Just around the doorframe, I saw Jack forcing an uncomfortable smile. His eyes met mine and the tension in his jaw suddenly disappeared.

"Yeah, nice to finally meet you, too," he returned to Ian, shaking his hand, then took a hesitant step over the threshold. "Sorry I'm late, I couldn't find my tie."

"I've got some you can borrow," Ian turned on his heel and pegged it up the stairs to his room, tripping multiple times on the way up.

I let out an awkward laugh and gave Jack a small wave.

"Hi."

"Hello."

Amarra coughed into the rim of her coffee mug.

"Sorry. Jack, this is Amarra. Amarra, Jack."

"Dead brave thing you're doing facing the Fallon clan. I only managed one Christening before I swore I'd never brave them again."

"Amarra," I warned as I turned to grab my case. She ignored me and gave Jack one of her charming smiles, dimples and all.

"Mel's family can be *overwhelming,* that's for sure," Amarra teased from behind her coffee. "Hope you know what you're setting yourself up for."

"I'm sure I've been to worse social events," Jack reassured. "Award shows, for a start, are a nightmare. I mean, the first one I ever went to, the only person I knew was one of the bartenders, from school."

Amarra nodded along, amused she was even pretending she could relate to such a statement. "Well, yeah... I mean, sure."

"I thought you went to your first award show with the whole *Violins* cast?" I teased, rolling my case towards the front door. "How can you say you *only* knew the bartender?"

"First time I went I was a seat-filler. I'll take that for you." He lifted my case effortlessly over the threshold and carried it to the boot of his car. "You know one of those people that sits in a celebrity's seat while they're in the toilet or at the bar, so the audience still looks full?"

"Such humble beginnings," Amarra mused, nudging me out the door. "God, he's fitter than you said," she whispered in my ear.

I coughed loudly, choking on my own breath. Thankfully, Jack hadn't heard her — he was too distracted by Ian tumbling manically down the stairs.

"Right," Ian began, "I've got patterned, non-patterned, luminous, sequined, tribal, and textured. Oh, and this one—" he raised one of the many ties draped over his arm, "—glows in the dark!"

Jack shot me a desperate look. "Mel?"

"Oh, I'd go for the glow-in-the-dark, no question about it."

Clearly me teasing him made the decision somewhat less intimidating. "I'll just take the plain dark blue one, please."

"Are you gonna be wearing a dark blue suit? Because you don't want to go matchy-matchy, do you? Go for the burgundy." Ian thrust said burgundy tie towards him. "Or I have a few dickie bows that could work!"

Jack quickly took the offered tie. "Na, this one's great. Thanks, Ian. Mel, you ready?"

"Yeah, sure," I felt myself say, though I was screaming internally. *No.* I was not ready. Packed, yes, but not mentally prepared for this mind boggling escapade — not one bit.

Amarra pulled me in for one last squeeze. She pecked my burning hot cheek and whispered, "If you don't try and shag him, I might just have to have a go at it myself."

I was so absorbed by Amarra I hadn't even noticed Ian had followed Jack to the driver's side door and was talking his ear off. Jack was staring at me with panic behind his eyes, begging to be rescued.

Guess we're both the damsel in distress.

"Come on, Ian," I said, pulling at the back of his collar. "We have a plane to catch."

Ian nodded, giddy. "Private? I'm sure you have a private plane, Jack? Is it one of those where you get to face the other way?"

I pinched Ian's elbow subtly, but he yelped. He glared at me and rubbed his arm resentfully. He no doubt thought it was his hot minute to try and be Jack's new BFF.

"See you when I get back, Ian."

I gave him a half-hearted hug.

"Send me lots of pics," he hissed, "especially if he gets his top off!"

I rolled my eyes and clambered into the car. As Jack drove down the uneven, pothole-ridden drive, I looked back through the side view mirror and saw Ian and Amarra, waving like maniacs. Thankfully, Jack was too busy concentrating on the road to notice — or too kind to give away the fact that he had.

The drive to the airport was painfully silent. It reminded me of the first time we met, only now I wasn't cocky, confident and unaware of Jack's favourite colour. I was on edge, knowing I was going to be spending almost a week playing make-believe with a guy who I'd kissed twice, and insulted more times than I'd care to mention.

We didn't say anything remotely noteworthy to one another until we were actually sitting side by side on the plane. Up until that point, all Jack had really said to me was, 'What gate?', 'Got your ticket?', 'Let me carry your case for you', and 'Fancy anything to eat?'.

How had I suddenly become such an awful conversationalist? It was dire. I feared we were going to spend the next five days like this.

"So, how come your folks are in France?" Jack asked, not making eye contact as he attempted to untangle his headphones. *He's going to zone out the whole flight and just listen to music? Good idea.*

"Well, they're out there because Dad had sort of a mid-life crisis thing really," I reached for my bag buried under the seat in front. "Most blokes buy a supercar, Dad went for the Vineyard instead."

"He has a *vineyard*? Jesus."

"Don't be too impressed, he can't make wine — like, *at all*."

Jack laughed.

"No, seriously. He tried making a bottle the first year he moved and honestly, it was like treacle. He employs people to make it now. He doesn't take part, or make any decisions, just drinks the final result and calls it all a job well done."

"Sounds like he's living the dream."

I rolled my eyes. The amount of times I'd heard that.

"How did he get that round your mum? A mid-life crisis like that," Jack laughed heartily. "Coming home with a new shiny sports car — yeah, you can explain it to the missus. Tell her it makes you feel young again. But a vineyard? I imagine she had a lot to say about that."

"Not really," I mused to myself. "She didn't say a word."

"Really?"

"Well, no, being dead and all."

Jack blinked.

"I thought you said your mum was out there with him?"

"She is," I chuckled. "In an urn, on the mantelpiece."

Jack swore under his breath, but eventually I saw the smallest of smiles break the surface.

"You really set me up for that one."

"I've been doing it to pretty much everyone since the day she died. It takes the edge off the subject. Don't take it personally."

"*Oh, God,*" Jack sunk into his chair and stared blankly out of the tiny window. Eventually his eyes crinkled and an embarrassed laugh broke out. "I feel like such a dick."

"Why?"

He shook his head at me and there was something so innocent about his laughter that my heart lurched forward. "I've been full on preparing to meet both your parents. Had compliments and lines ready and everything. I feel like a right pillock." He shook his head again.

Meet the parents. God, he really was starting to get into the role of 'fake boyfriend' — and taking it seriously, too. Maybe he saw this as an acting gig? *Something to reconnect him with his craft?* I sniggered to myself.

We landed in Marseille Airport, Dad meeting us at arrivals. He gave me his usual teddy bear, lasts-too-long hug. Jack got a stern handshake.

"Nice to finally meet you, Jack," Dad said, cheerily. "I would say I've heard so much about you, but in all honesty, Mel hasn't told me a thing. She's only really said that everything in the press about you and her is completely and utterly made-up, which I'm now starting to question considering you're here as her plus-one. So, are you dating my daughter or not?"

My jaw dropped slightly.

"We haven't really put a label on it, Mr Bishop."

"A label? What are ye', a jar of jam?"

I grimaced, "Please don't make this harder than it needs to be."

"As the actress said to the Bishop," Dad joked.

Oh God, this was *so* not the time for Dad to be himself.

"Well, it's good to have you, Jack. Even if you guys haven't labelled whatever *this is* yet."

I cringed even more, my stomach twisting into knots. I sent pleading glances to my dad in the hope he would, for the love of God, stop talking before he made it worse.

"You've done Mel a big favour by coming. She usually just sits by the pool, bored and twiddling her thumbs when she visits, but with you here, she'll finally have someone to play with!"

... And he made it worse.

We all crammed into Dad's beaten-up classic yellow Mini and spent the whole drive to the villa in awkward silence — made worse by the thick, stale air as Dad still hadn't had the air-con fixed. There were a few comments about the stunning scenery, the nice weather, and the prospect of Dad hosting so many people over the next couple of days.

"I'm taking it one day at a time," Dad said, pulling up to the pebbled drive. "I'm sure when everyone starts arriving I'll probably start to feel it, but today, I'm relaxed. I'm calm. I'm happy."

"That's a very good way to live your life, Ted," Jack agreed, trailing off as soon as the villa came into view. I didn't blame him, it didn't matter how many times I saw this place, every time felt like the first.

It really was a pocket of paradise. It was old and quirky, like my dad. It had a few cracks here and there, but the view made up for that. Dad had the entire valley outside his front door, stretching out and leading down to the vineyard. It was breathtaking and heartbreaking at the same time. First time I'd seen it, Dad sat me on the vine-infested stone wall that circled the grounds and said, "Best view in the world, Mel, but still a world without your mum."

While Dad and Jack brought the bags in, I snuck my way into the front room. There, a soft-cinnamon-coloured, full-bodied orb of an urn was waiting for me.

"Hiya, Mum," I said, stepping towards the mantelpiece and running my finger across the curved edge of the lid. "Sorry it's been so long."

My eyes glanced across the date. It had been almost three years since her passing, but part of me still felt like it was yesterday. That sad, silly, grieving part of me that yearned for just one more hug. One more poorly made cup of tea. One last well-meaning yet terrible piece of advice.

"How have you been?"

I was met with expected silence.

"Now, don't flip your lid, but I may have brought a boy with me," I whispered, unable to hold back the smile on my face. "He's nothing like the last one, don't worry. He's called Jack and he's an actor."

I knew Mum would object to that so I quickly added, "*Don't start,*" before continuing: "It's not serious, before you ask, it's just to wind up Willow. Jack's not really the dating type — unless it helps elevate his career." I rolled my eyes. *How's your career?* Mum would no doubt ask.

I bit the inside of my cheek. My career was always a touchy subject with Mum. It's not that she wasn't supportive, she just saw me going down a different path.

"*I know, I know* — I should've been a midwife. Despite the fact I hate blood, I don't do well in hospitals - *your fault* - and I don't really like babies, to be honest," I laughed, imagining somewhere in the far distance I could hear Mum laughing, too.

There was no laugh, just the distant chatter of Dad and Jack somewhere in the house. "Well, I'd better join them before Dad starts showing Jack my baby photos. Or worse — *his own.*"

9th June

Anyone who knows me knows that I'm a slut for an all butter croissant. I'm a slut for most pastries, to be honest...

Dad had made it very clear — Jack and I were to be in separate rooms, on opposite sides of the house. Not because he was a prude, he just wanted us to have the best rooms during our stay.

My room was my usual — ensuite bathroom and a view overlooking the pool, which is normally quite pleasant, only today Jack decided to go for an early-morning swim and all of a sudden it became torture.

All I'd done was stick my head out of the window when I'd heard a splash of water. I expected it to be a stray cat having accidentally fallen in, not a half-naked Jack. I hid behind the sheer net curtain and watched him do laps, considering Ian's request to take photos. I didn't, *obviously.*

Jack emerged from the back door, a tray of croissants in one hand, a glass jug of orange juice in the other. He winked at me as he placed the tray down in front of Dad.

Jack filled my glass and sat beside me, his hand ever so briefly touching my thigh. *Just an accident,* I told myself. *Don't overthink it, or you're not going to make it through the next five minutes, let alone the next five days.*

"Is this homemade jam?" Jack asked, picking up the glowing red jar with my mum's handwriting scrawled across its label. *Crab Apple.* "You didn't strike me as a jam maker, Ted," Jack said, innocently, scooping out a dollop.

Dad's eyes met mine from across the table as we shared a sorrowful moment.

I cleared my throat, uncomfortable.

"Freckle's mum made it," Dad explained. "She had an allotment round the back of our old house. Made thousands of jars, as she sold them at markets. But since she passed, we couldn't shift them. So, I've just had a constant supply." He pointed at the half-empty jar and sighed. "Only got five jars left…"

Jack looked at the oversized blob on the side of his plate regretfully.

I gave his hand a reassuring squeeze. "Give over with that look. Mum wanted it eaten."

When I withdrew my hand, he gripped hold of it and linked his fingers between mine. I looked down at them, for a second not knowing which were his and which were mine.

The sound of tyres fighting against grit broke the moment between us. A small silver car struggled to get up the drive. The flash of blonde hair in the passenger's seat made my heart sink.

Cousin Willow.

"God, she's here," I turned to my dad, panic stricken. "You said she wasn't coming till this evening!" I snatched my hand away from Jack and ran my fingers through my hair, trying to flatten it as best I could. The humidity had not been kind. I desperately rummaged through my pockets for a bobble.

"Mel? What are you doing?" Jack's eyebrows furrowed.

"Just trying to find a—" I heard the car doors bang open. "For God's sake, I haven't even prepped you. Just try not to hate me when you meet her. Like, I did try to warn you my family was mad and Willow, she has this nickname for me—"

"*Little Nips!*"

My two most hated words cut through the villa grounds like a crack of thunder.

Dad arose from his seat, throwing me a deeply apologetic glance.

Too late to feel sorry for me now, old man, I thought.

"Uncle Teddy, you look so tanned!" Willow threw her arms around Dad and squeezed the breath out of him. Dad's face scrunched with pain. "Thank you again for letting us do this! Honestly, if there was any other way we could have—" Willow waved at the shell of a man who was only just emerging from the driver's side. "Gareth! Come and meet Uncle Teddy. And Lil' Nips is here too, with…"

Willow froze.

"Jack," my dad finished for her, completely oblivious to Willow's internal breakdown. "Mel's plus-one. You did say she could bring someone."

Jack gave a short, confident wave before placing his arm on the back of my chair and leaning a little closer into me. He was playing this part better than most of his film roles.

"Nice to meet you, Willow."

She blinked her new false eyelashes and let out a puff of disbelief. "But, I—"

Gareth fought with three large suitcases to eventually shake Dad's hand. "Lovely to finally meet you, Uncle Teddy."

"Oh, that nickname is catching on is it? *Magic,*" Dad pursed his lips. "Let me help you with those."

"Oh, thanks. Got six more in the car," Gareth laughed awkwardly.

Jack jumped up and gave me a quick, brief kiss on the cheek. "I better lend a hand or your dad's gonna put his back out."

"I heard that!" Dad barked, grinning widely.

Jack chuckled, jogging over to the car and side-stepping Willow, who was still frozen to the spot.

All three men heaved the copious amounts of luggage up the cracked stone front steps. Once inside, Willow shot me a look, eyes burning with jealous fury.

"*Jack Hart?*"

I shrugged and sipped my orange juice smugly. "Who else did you expect me to bring?"

Willow had managed to get her acrylic nails into Jack faster than you could say *jealous bridezilla*. She'd roped him into setting up chairs, hanging up banners, making up favours. Anything at all that meant he was by her side, and not mine. How Gareth was keeping a cool lid on was beyond me. I felt like a whistling kettle about to boil over, and Jack wasn't even my real boyfriend, let alone my fiancé.

Right before dinner, I finally got a moment alone with Jack. I could do nothing but apologise.

"It's fine," Jack reassured me, "I've been around clingier women, I'm used to it."

I rolled my eyes, amused. Before, that would have ruffled my feathers. I would've thought, 'How dare Jack think he was so fit that women fawn over him?' But now, I got it. I could acknowledge that, yes, Jack was fit, and women did fall over him. Willow included.

"Did you bring your diary with you, Freckles?" Dad asked, coming into the kitchen for some cutlery. "Or has bringing a fella meant you've had to make some luggage changes?"

"Dad..."

"She always brings her diary, Jack. Wherever she goes. Writes, writes, writes."

"Mel has mentioned she's a writer. Got a play that you're finalising, haven't you?"

I glared at Jack, my dad suddenly gasping with joy.

"Really? That's amazing!" Dad squeezed me, knives and forks clinking and clanking in my ear as he wiggled me back and forth. "Blummin' brilliant that you're getting back into it!"

I patted Dad's shoulder and gently pushed him off of me. This was the side of Dad I loved and hated in equal measure. The overly supportive parent who puts you on a pedestal, so that your inevitable fall from grace and failure will be all the more devastating.

"She used to write stories all the time when she was little, Jack. They were about fairies, and goblins at the bottom of the garden. She used to make me take the scribbled pages into the office to get them laminated — then it all stopped. School and boys, acting and London. You know how it is."

My cheeks felt like they were about to melt off of my face. Dad continued, oblivious.

"So, go on, what's it about?" he asked eagerly.

"It's nothing, Dad, really..."

"About a woman at a crossroads, isn't it, Mel? Still in a love triangle, or have you decided to write what you know yet?" Jack teased, not reading my face well at all.

"I don't know much," I replied, Dad now staring at me with wonder and pride. "So, that doesn't leave me with much to work with."

"You could write about your mum," Dad interrupted. "You'd have plenty of material."

"Write a morbid play about Mum's death? *Oh, I'd love to,*" I scoffed. "Hold on, let me grab a pen."

"Not her death," Dad frowned, not picking up on any of my sarcasm. "I mean, you should write about her life, your relationship — all those conversations you had while you waited for Monday."

Jack shot me a curious look. I swallowed the lump in my throat, ignored him and prayed for him not to ask.

"Waited for Monday?"

My prayers go unanswered yet again, I internally screamed.

Dad beamed, "Oh, it's this phrase Freckles and her mum came up with when we got the terminal prognosis. You'd just dropped out of drama school, hadn't you? To help me take care of her. They both decided that they would spend whatever time they had left together. End-of-life care their way. And amongst all of their conversations they came up with this analogy: that waiting for death is like waiting for Monday. It's inevitable. But before you know it, it's Tuesday. Have I got that right, Freckles?"

I nodded weakly, "Yeah, something like that."

"You should write about that!" Dad jingled the cutlery, excited. "I think it'll be a beautiful little insight into what it's like losing someone to cancer. It could help a lot of people. So many people go through it."

"It's definitely common," Jack added softly. No doubt he was thinking about his grandad.

"You could have a tonne of people going to see your play, and leave knowing that they're not alone."

"It's a play that's needed, Dad, sure," I stammered. "But I don't think I'm the one to write it."

"Don't be ridiculous!" Dad laughed heartily. "Stop quitting on yourself before you've even started and crack on."

I didn't see Dad leave the room as my head was in my hands. I just heard the rattle of cutlery, and the back door slam shut.

Two hands gingerly swept down my arms and took hold of my wrists. Jack was kneeling down in front of me; a sad, apologetic, puppy expression across his face.

"I'm sorry, I wouldn't have asked if I'd known."

I shrugged. "It is what it is."

"I don't think your dad realised he was being pushy—"

"He wasn't. He was being supportive, in his own weird way." I considered why Dad had been more encouraging than usual. "Jack, he's been wanting me to talk about Mum for ages."

"Why haven't you?"

I pulled a face. "Are you seriously asking me that?" I groaned. "The *material* he's talking about—"

The image of Mum's face twisted in pain clogged my vision. I no longer saw Jack sympathetically staring at me, but Mum in her hospital bed, pinned down by four nurses, screaming.

"I can't write about Mum," I whispered, the image fading. "We went through too much."

"Writing it down could help you process it."

"I don't want to process it, Jack. I don't want to even think about it."

Jack kissed my forehead, and it was only then that I realised I was crying. Of all the people I didn't want to cry in front of, Jack was definitely top of the list.

"I think," Jack said, squeezing my hands, "you can write about it, but only when you're ready. Grieving takes time. Three years, or thirty years, it makes no difference." He kissed the backs of my hands, and then gingerly kissed the inside of my wrists. "I'll help you in whatever way I can, okay? Whatever I can do to support you. God knows I'm going to need the favour returned when my grandad goes." He straightened up and pulled me onto my feet. "Come on, Freckles, let's get some food."

I thumped him, half blubbering, half laughing. "Don't start calling me that."

10th June

Family occasions have a scary resemblance to school trips to the zoo.

The cavalry arrived in full force. Nana Tia and Gramps came first. Nana was wearing an inappropriately large hat, bitching and moaning about the French-speaking taxi driver from the moment she stepped foot out of the car.

"Why can't they just learn English?" she scoffed.

"Because we're in France, woman! He's French, let him speak his own damn language, in his own damn country!" Gramps barked, passing the driver a generous, and no doubt apology-filled, tip. "Now, get ya bag before I throw it in' pool!"

Nana spotted Jack from a mile away and was soon reviewing him from over the top of her bejewelled sunglasses.

"So, that's your new man, is it?" she asked me, both of us watching him deal with another one of Willow's frivolous wedding requests.

"Sort of," I replied.

Nana shot me a sideways glance. "What do you mean, *sort of*? What kind of an answer is that, 'sort of'? He either is or he isn't."

"Okay, then," I confidently replied, eager to get Jack's and my fake relationship plan well and truly underway. "He is my new man."

"Hmph," Nana pouted. "Your Auntie Angela says he's an actor as well?" she rolled her eyes and pushed her sunglasses back up her nose. "Just what we need, another *actor* in the family."

Gramps lit up a cigarette, using my back as a wind cover. "Ignore the wench," he whispered, before straightening. "Is he any good?"

"What kind of a question is that?" Nana scoffed at him, "Doesn't matter if he's any good. How much does he earn, Melissa? What does he hold in his estate? That's how you know if a man is good material or not. Can't provide for a family by being good at anything — *especially* acting!"

I considered, at that point, whether or not to tell Nana that Jack's net worth was about seven and a half million pounds. *It could give her the heart attack we've all been waiting for.*

At the rehearsal dinner, Jack well and truly earned his stay by keeping his arm firmly around my waist. He was my perfect, chiselled, and talented force field, batting off every backhanded compliment that got thrown my way.

"So how's the acting hobby going, Mel? Finally making it past the audition stages?"

"Actually, Kenneth, Sir, Mel has been juggling auditions, press for our most recent film *Symbol of Freedom*, and her already hectic work schedule, quite successfully. She's even thinking of branching out into writing, broadening her horizons and maximising her opportunities."

"I can't believe Mel's actually managed to tie someone down. We always hear about possible boyfriends but then never meet them. Makes you start to wonder if any of them were real."

"I can assure you, Angela, I'm very much real. Can I get you another pinot?"

I might have to book Jack to be my fake boyfriend again for Christmas. It was turning out to be the best idea anyone had ever had. I was starting to — dare I say — enjoy myself. That was until Willow began hitting her champagne glass with her fork.

Our entire family, sitting around the gigantic garden table, looked up at her.

"Family and friends," she chimed, clearing her throat, "I know it's not usually tradition for the bride to make a speech, but I thought, screw that! It's my rehearsal dinner, and I have a few words."

Her eyes then flickered my way and I felt my stomach churn. She was plotting something, and there was nothing I could do to stop it.

"Firstly, I want to thank our gorgeous host, Uncle Teddy."

Dad smiled shyly from behind his wine glass.

"To welcome us all into your home, after everything you and Lil' Nips—" Willow sniggered, "—I mean, Lil' Mel, have gone through, is just so amazing. We all miss Auntie Theresa."

Everyone froze.

No one said her name. Not ever. It was just 'Mum', 'my mum', 'our mum', 'yer mum' — never *Theresa*. I immediately looked at Gramps, who was gripping so tightly onto his glass, his knuckles had gone white. He was no doubt having the same involuntary response as me.

Out of the corner of my eye I noticed my dad had started to shuffle uncomfortably in his chair.

Dad never had an issue talking about Mum, he almost took comfort in it, but hearing her name might've been a step too far for him as well.

"She was a joy in all our lives and to die so young, it really was a tragedy. But *everything happens for a reason*, as they say, and if Auntie Theresa hadn't passed on, we wouldn't be here today, would we?"

I think I'm going to be sick, I thought, bile creeping up my throat. *No way was Willow bringing this up now.*

"Uncle Teddy wouldn't have his villa, would he? And then we'd all probably be in the local cricket club or something!"

There could have been laughter but I wasn't sure. It all sounded like white noise as I stared at my dad across the table, who was slowly sinking into his chair. He wouldn't make eye contact with me. He wouldn't look up at all.

"A beautiful place that I'm sure cost a bob or—"

Gramps stood up, his chair scraping against the flags. "To Theresa," he grunted, lifting his Champagne glass. "I think that's what you're getting at. Eh, Willow?"

Willow fluttered her eyelashes, tipsy. "Ah, yes, sorry. Thank you, Gramps. Let's all raise a glass and remember our Theresa."

Glasses raised. Family members drank, and as conversations began to pick up again, Dad subtly excused himself and scuttled off towards the kitchen. I followed, ignoring Jack's questionable gaze as I got up from the table.

"Dad?" I asked, coming through the back door. "Are you okay?"

I found him by the sink, sipping a glass of water.

"I'm fine," he reassured. "Wine's just hit me, I think."

He finally looked up at me, his tears magnified by the lens of his glasses. "I think I'm going to head up to bed. Can you let them all know when you go back out?"

"Dad..."

"Goodnight, Freckles," he planted a tear-stained, loving kiss on my cheek. "I love you, you know?"

"I know. I love you, too."

With my toes in the pool, knees up to my chest, and sunscreen burning my eyes, I heard footsteps crunching against the pebbled path. I didn't have to look to know Jack had come to find me. *Do I really know the sound of his footsteps already?*

"Was wondering where you'd disappeared off to," he chuckled, removing his shoes and dunking his feet into the crystal clear water.

"Yeah, sorry I needed some air," I rubbed my temples.

"You know you were already outside, right?" Jack chuckled.

"I mean air without relatives," I grunted. "They've given me a headache."

"Your cousin Willow is... *interesting*."

"Oh, she's a delight."

Jack smiled apologetically. God, this was torment. Why had I dragged him here? Why had I even agreed to come here myself? It wasn't as though I'd ever thought this was going to be fun. I should have just declined the invite and suffered the consequences. It would've been less painful.

"Let me help with that."

Suddenly, I felt Jack's hand weave itself under my mass of frazzled hair. His fingers skated across the top of my spine and, before I knew it, his right thumb began tracing a figure of eight deep into my skin. I only just managed to stop a moan from parting my lips.

"That's..."

"Helping relieve the headache?"

I'll say.

My toes were starting to curl. *When had this swimming pool started to boil?* I bit my lip to stop myself from asking him to try that massaging motion of his thumb elsewhere. *Oh, God, even the thought...*

His hand fell from my neck. Why was he stopping? What had I done? I realised my eyes were closed and looked his way. Jack was hunched over, busy watching his own feet paddling in the water.

"Has she always been that way with you?"

Oh right, Willow. *Yeah, that's a turn-off for sure.*

I wet both my hands in the pool and ran my fingers through my hair trying to flatten some of the frizz. I cleared my throat before answering, "I feel like she's branded me *Lil' Nips* for the rest of my life."

"I've been meaning to ask how that nickname came about."

I rolled my eyes, the memory a distant, yet still triggering, haze. "It was my Auntie Angela's 40th, for like the third year in a row. I would've been about thirteen and my boobs were just starting to come in. I hadn't had time to go shopping for a training bra. So, I went braless to this birthday party, wearing this bottle green tank dress, and when there was a gust of wind, I got cold. My nipples just poked through this dress like bad mosquito bites. Cut to ten or so years later, and she's *still* calling me Lil' Nips."

Jack half smiled, giving it a minute before giving in to what he actually wanted to talk about.

"Your dad didn't come back to dinner, is he okay?"

I shrugged. "I hope so."

"Was it the mention of your mum that set him off?"

"No," I breathed. "If you hadn't noticed, Dad loves talking about Mum. It's just..." I grit my teeth together. "There's always been this ongoing judgement on Mum's side of the family that Dad bought this place with her money. That's what Willow meant about not being here if Mum hadn't died. It was a dig at my dad."

I shook my head, still baffled that Willow'd actually done it.

"Mum didn't have any money. Dad sold his business, and my childhood home, and bought this place all within the first year of Mum being gone. A lot of people round that table back there got jealous about it. Hated him for doing it. Even rang him and told him."

The same image of Mum's twisted face appeared in my mind again. Lying in her hospital bed, pinned down by nurses, Dad wide-eyed and traumatised in the corner.

"They've no idea what Dad and I went through. He needed this place... It saved him."

Jack had gone still, staring at me, concern etched across his face.

"What was your mum like?"

Radged, I thought. *Like the rest of us.*

"Mum was—" I tried to find the right words. When had I last talked, *really talked*, about my mum? "She was an artist before anything else. It even seeped into her parenting. Like, I grew up not being allowed to use erasers because I needed to learn to 'live and work with my mistakes'. She loved food — cheese and bread more than anything. Very eclectic taste in music; one minute you'd be listening to rhythm and blues, then musical theatre, then punk rock to finish. She had a great sense of humour. Found me funny. God knows why — all I do is chat bollocks," I gestured to my own mouth, aware I was rambling. "Point proven."

"She sounds like she was a wonderful woman."

"She was a pain in the arse, Jack. But she was my mum and I loved her."

"How did she cope with all of them?" Jack threw a thumb towards the distant chatter. No doubt Gramps would be trying to make a ciggy escape, Nana Tia would be chastising some poor sod, and Willow would probably be cheating on her fiancé with an usher or two.

"She didn't," I laughed. "Mum struggled the same as the rest of us with their antics, so most of the time she just kept her distance from them. Suppose that paid off in the end, didn't hurt her when none of them came to see her on her deathbed. Except Gramps," I scoffed. "Want to know what Uncle Kenneth's response was when Mum told him she had terminal cancer? 'Oh sis, I thought I'd die first'."

I couldn't help but laugh through the pain, wiping a stray tear away with the back of my hand. "Anyway," I diverted. "How're you coping with them all?"

"Your nana keeps squeezing my arm and calling me *Jack Hart*," Jack confessed, visibly grimacing.

I felt myself prickle, still laughing. "Well that's what happens when you have a name, Jack. People tend to use it."

"You know what I mean," he splashed some water at me playfully. I pushed him away, my hand probably lingering far too long on his arm. "She's double barrelling me. I don't know whether she's coming on to me, or about to give me a bollocking."

"I don't want to even think about my nana coming on to you, thanks."

Jack laughed, "I wouldn't even try it with her, Mel. Your grandad could definitely take me."

I hummed in agreement.

Jack laughed and I felt the urge to kiss him. Wondered if I leaned towards him, would he lean the rest of the way? *Should I try it?* It would've definitely made me feel better, and we were trying to be a convincing couple after all... Before I had another moment to think about it further, I suddenly felt the sting of chlorine flood my nose. Jack had pushed me and thrown himself into the pool.

We made our way back to the house, piss wet through, leaving two snail trails of pool water behind us. We snuck in through the kitchen and up the back stairs. As our rooms were in separate directions we parted ways on the landing. I turned to head to my room, starting to feel a bit of a chill through my damp clothes, when Jack's fingers suddenly wrapped around my wrist.

"I'll see you for the big day, tomorrow then," he said.

It could have been the heat or the lingering smell of chlorine clouding my judgement, but I could've sworn he was leaning in.

"What the hell have you two been doin'?" Gramps bellowed, coming out of the bathroom, adjusting his belt beneath his pot belly. "Fall in t'bog or what?"

Jack took a swift step back and feigned a laugh. "No, Mr Fallon. Had a bit of a tumble into the pool, I'm afraid."

Gramps raised an eyebrow, "Both of yers?"

"Jack first, I went in after," I teased. "Jack can't swim, you see."

Jack threw me an embarrassed glare but begrudgingly went along with my lie. "Yeah, never learnt, unfortunately."

Gramps *humfed* disapprovingly, leaning close to me. "That's not natural, Mel. All that money and he never thought to get himself some swimming lessons." Gramps headed downstairs with another disapproving *humf*.

Jack and I were alone once again, but the 'could-have-been' moment had very much gone.

"Night, Jack."

"Night, Mel."

11th June

Ladies and Gentlemen, family of the bride and groom, we are gathered here today to celebrate the love of... A lass who just wanted an excuse to wear an extortionately-priced dress, and a lad stupid enough to believe this marriage is going to last longer than a year.

I thought I'd seen Jack at his sexiest in his fighter pilot uniform, but then he opened his bedroom door, and I was left speechless by the vision of him in his suit. A dark blue tux, crisp white shirt, buttons undone to reveal a smooth, hairless torso. *Did he get a wax...?* I tried to keep my eyes focused on something above shoulder height to avoid reaching out and running my fingers over his bare skin.

"You about ready?" I swallowed.

Jack was blinking back at me, a shoe in one hand, the door handle in the other. "Mel, you look—"

"Stupid, I know. It's Amarra's dress so not really my thing, but hey-ho. It'll have to do."

Jack nodded slowly, allowing his eyes to roam up and down my body. *Was the fit really that bad?* I thought, patting down the front of the dress self-consciously.

"You want to come in?" He finally fixed his eyes on my face. "I'll be a few minutes, so you might as well."

I shrugged and he stepped aside to let me pass.

Dad had a few guest rooms, but the one Jack was staying in was particularly sweet. Sheer curtains over double French windows, pale blue walls and a fluffy, soft carpet you could scrunch your toes into.

"Enjoying the shagpile?"

Jack shut the door with a laugh. "Say again?"

"The carpet, it's *shagpile*, not that you can see it—" I tread carefully around the exploded contents of Jack's suitcase.

"Yeah it's nice." He sat on the end of the bed beside me and pulled on his missing shoe. "So, how are we playing today — same as last night? Or are you wanting a full-on boyfriend/girlfriend performance? Really try and get the bride's blood boiling?"

I laughed nervously. "You sound like you're going to start asking me for a full character breakdown in a minute."

Jack tied his laces, his knee up to his chest. "I'm just wanting to know the parameters before I end up getting in trouble for doing something you're not happy with."

"Like what?" I asked, dumbly.

"Well," Jack straightened, "how much physical intimacy are you wanting? If you want us to be believable as a couple, I'm guessing you're going to want me to kiss you."

Yes please, thank you very much, please, I thought. *Snog my face off, Mr Hart.*

"I mean..." I took a breath, trying to pass off my complete brain malfunction as a possible sneeze. "That could — yeah, but I—" I no longer had the ability to put words together, just noises. "Sure?"

Jack's eyebrows raised, "Are you sure you're sure? You hesitated."

"Only because..." I began, wondering how I could complete the sentence without saying something like, '*You caught me off guard, you dickwad.*' "I needed a moment to think about it first," I finished.

"What's there to think about?" Jack fretted. "It's not like we haven't kissed before." He stood and began to button up his shirt.

I felt my eyes bulge, thrown. *Was he seriously bringing that up now?*

Jack casually checked his reflection in the large mirror hanging on the wall. "Though, I suppose they were different. Very alcohol influenced, what with you being pretty pissed in Manchester, and me having had a few at the wrap party."

"True," I considered. "Though, in fairness, I don't see myself staying sober past the vows today."

I glanced at Jack's reflection, curious to know what he was thinking, and saw he was beaming from ear to ear.

"What are you looking at me like that for?"

"Just nice to know you *do* actually remember kissing me in Manchester..."

My mouth suddenly went dry. I felt myself blush, confident Jack wouldn't be able to tell considering how sunburnt my cheeks were.

I jumped to my feet, desperate to get out of the room. "God, we're going to be late if you don't get a wiggle on. Shall I meet you downstairs? I'll meet you downstairs," I scurried towards the door not wanting to give him the chance to respond.

"Mel," Jack laughed, placing his hands firmly on my waist and holding me still. "I'm taking the piss."

I felt a soft, affectionate, brief kiss on my forehead.

"You don't half overthink, you know?" Jack chuckled, releasing me and grabbing Ian's burgundy tie from the bed. "So that's a yes to the kissing. It'll help to make it believable, and we'll be a convincing couple. But let's not overdo it, so we don't ruin our friendship, yeah?"

Friendship.

I'm glad he clarified that. No, really, I am. Not disappointed at all. It meant I could get through the day without thinking anything Jack did romantically towards me was real. It meant no lines were going to be crossed and I could, for once, not *overthink* everything.

Jack lifted his tie towards me, "Can you help me with this? I've always been useless with them."

"Sure."

Don't remember the wedding, only remember wine, dancing, and *kissing*. Lots and lots of kissing. Did I mention wine? Now — I need to find Jack's room.

12th June

The best decisions are made when you're drunk at ten past three in the morning... No, wait.

I may have out done myself on the self-destructive front. I could've easily left things at a mess-free, all-time high. But no, I just couldn't help myself, could I?

I wobbled across the landing, and all the way to Jack's bedroom at stupid o'clock in the morning and knocked. There was no answer. *Maybe he's fallen asleep?* I thought. It wouldn't surprise me. He was probably exhausted, having spent the entire day playing 'boyfriend' — and successfully, too. Everyone had believed it, even Willow. God, it was priceless. Everyone had admired Jack more than her dress, congratulated me on my successful 'catch' before congratulating the bride and groom. It was hard not to feel smug all day, comforted by the thought that Willow would definitely think twice before assigning me a plus-one at her next wedding.

I knocked again. There was no answer. I retreated, confident Jack wasn't coming to the door, only to suddenly bump into him standing right behind me.

"What are you doing?" His eyes scanned my face so intensely I couldn't even begin to think up a lie. *Would 'I've run out of toothpaste' work?*

"I was just—" my words caught in my throat. His white shirt was unbuttoned again, the smell of wine lingering on his breath. "Wait — Never mind me, what are *you* doing?"

Panic flashed in his eyes, then a drunk sort of wonky smile appeared.

"I've just been knocking on *your* bedroom door," Jack confessed.

"Why?"

"Why the hell do you think?"

Jack's lips were suddenly on mine, his hands on my waist, my back pressed hard against his bedroom door. He groaned as I instinctively bit his lip. My knees almost buckled as his fingers gripped onto my hips. I couldn't believe it was happening. Adamant God was either making up for all the times he'd screwed me over, or all the alcohol I'd drunk was causing me to have a very vivid hallucination.

Jack jiggled the door handle and we both stumbled back into the room. He pressed his weight against me, and we landed loudly against the wall. Suspending both my wrists above my head with one hand, his other teased the hem of my dress, his fingertips skating up my thigh.

"What do you want, Mel?"

My mind was rattled, and my thoughts scrambled. It was an easy question to answer, I wanted *him*, but I struggled to find the courage to say it. It was then that I realised I could feel his heart beating just as fast as mine.

"You. I want *you*."

"Thank God," he moaned, almost taking a chunk of skin off my shoulder. He kissed the length of my collarbone. Then his lips made their way down my body, and under my dress.

I felt myself quiver, my breath catch. My fingers scrunched his hair tightly.

Jack stood, grinning, before wrapping my legs around his waist and carrying me over to his bed. He was clearly a pro, a true expert in his craft. It made me wonder how many women he'd been with.

The roughness of his unshaved jaw pleasantly tickled my cheek. He took my dress and pulled it over my head. I saw his eyes scan over my body, his fingers itching to remove everything else.

I pulled his shirt off far too eagerly. Then his belt — bloody fiddly when you're pissed.

"Condom?" my brain panicked aloud. "God! I didn't bring any."

"S'okay," Jack panted, already wriggling out from under me. "I've got a pack in my case."

He reached for his bag and retrieved a box.

"You brought condoms?" I queried, smiling at him dopily. "A whole *box full?*"

It was hard not to laugh.

He looked back at me, the wrapper crinkling between his fingers, "A guy can dream can't he?" Jack slipped his right hand back into that comfortable spot around my waist and pulled me right on top of him. "Best dream I've ever had is *this*."

We were both limp. Breathless. Jack's hands still on my body, my arms around his neck. My legs were fully out for the count. Jack kissed me softly on the forehead, before getting up and heading for the bathroom. He didn't say a word, just shut the bathroom door behind himself and the room went silent. I felt myself curl up instinctively, all the ecstasy seeping out of me as I pulled the sheets up over myself.

I considered leaving, the reality of how stupid this spontaneous endeavour was had finally hit me.

Before I'd even removed the duvet, Jack had returned, grinning at me. I really had a chance to give his naked body the once over as he crossed the room. *I've just had that?* I thought, still not fully believing it.

Jack joined me under the covers, wrapping his arm around me and pulling me back to lie on top of him. With a satisfied grunt, he planted a kiss on my shoulder.

"We should do that more often," he chuckled, taking long, deep breaths.

The thought of doing it again, let alone *more often,* sent a tingling sensation down my spine. I tried to work out if Jack had meant this could even be something we did when we got back. The term *friends with benefits* came to mind.

He could just mean more often while we're here, I told myself. If that was the case, I was going to make good use of whatever time I had left.

My fingers started to skate across his torso, venturing wherever they pleased.

"I don't mean right this second, Mel. I need a minute to get my breath back."

"I didn't say anything."

Jack smirked, both his hands now resting behind his head. "Mmhmm..."

I kissed his chest and ran my fingers through his sweat soaked hair, pressing my weight against him.

"Mel..." Jack warned, playfully.

"I had to deal with you the other day. I say it's only fair."

His eyes widened. "What do you mean, *had to deal with me the other day*? What did I do?"

"Giving me that bloody massage," I chuckled into his neck, "I almost came right there by the pool."

Jack didn't laugh, which caught me off guard. Why wasn't he laughing? What I said was funny. Well, it was *supposed* to be funny.

"What're you looking at me like that for? I didn't come, just saying I nearly did, but then you stopped rubbing my neck—"

"I stopped because I'd got hard."

I burst out laughing.

"*You're kidding?*"

"No," he stated, stone faced, "I was just trying to help you with your headache, and then you went and started biting your lip and had this look on your face like you were gonna..."

"Come?" I sniggered.

Jack finally laughed along with me. He shook his head, dumbfounded, then wiped the sweat from his brow with the back of his hand. "So, you're telling me we could've been doing this all week?"

I kissed him delicately and took his bottom lip between my teeth. His whole body tensed beneath me as I kissed down his body.

"I said I needed a minute," he groaned, biting onto his fist. "You know, a minute? Sixty seconds? Then we can go—" he scrunched his eyes and growled. "God, you're a right chuffing pain in the arse."

Guess he didn't need a minute after all.

Jack's arms were quite firmly wrapped around me. Both of us were on our sides, the morning sunlight streaming in through the sheer curtains. Clothes had been thrown over every piece of furniture, the photos no longer straight, the bedside lamp knocked over on the floor.

It really happened.

But it was time for it to be over. Despite my desperation to snuggle closer to Jack, I knew that wasn't how friends with benefits worked. I needed to get out of there before he woke up. So, I lifted his arm and shimmied out of the bed.

A pale blue t-shirt was the closest thing in reach. I pulled it over my head, the scent of Jack filling my nostrils. Standing, I tiptoed towards the door, scanning the floor for my dress and shoes.

"I'm cold now," Jack grumbled into his pillow. "Get back here before I freeze."

I turned to find him half asleep, grumpily scowling at me. *Maybe he's still drunk?*

"I didn't know you were awake," I took a hesitant step back.

"I'm awake now. Where are you going?"

I racked my brain for a semi-believable excuse. "Just going to find some painkillers and try and have a shower, to be honest."

Jack stretched, yawning loudly before mischievously asking, "Is there room for two in that shower?"

My heart lurched. If this was still drunk Jack, or hungover Jack, or brain damaged Jack, it didn't really matter. I would be happy with any.

"Yeah," I laughed nervously. "Want to use your shower or mine?"

Jack, close behind, followed me down the stairs. We'd long missed breakfast, but with some wedding guests still knocking about I couldn't say I was sorry, just starving.

I grabbed Jack by the collar as we reached the hallway, pulling him close. I saw his neck was a bright collage of the night before.

"You trying to rip my shirt off?"

"There are relatives out there. We've got thirty seconds to grab as many croissants as we can before being seen. And I swear to God, if you waste any time grabbing fruit, I'll make you regret it. No one wants a pissin' orange when they're hungover."

"Fruit is sustenance, Mel. You're gonna need some if you want round two."

I sniggered. "Technically, it'd be round four."

"You're trying to kill me, woman."

The kitchen door swung open. Dad was on the other side holding a plate of pastries. "I thought I heard voices. What're you doing out here?"

"We were just—"

"Dilly dallying," Dad cut me off, "I'm going to have to reheat these now." Dad stood aside, wafting us into the kitchen. "Come on, come on, anyone would think you were hungover."

Jack gave me a knowing smile and headed for the porch where the breakfast table was waiting for him.

Dad watched him go, before turning to me with a disapproving look on his face. "You've absolutely destroyed that poor boy's neck."

Most of the family had left by noon, except for Nana Tia, Gramps, the newly-weds, and us. The lingering taste of alcohol meant everyone was on edge. Jack and I hadn't managed to get away, but instead had been forced to sit and socialise.

"You're quite the dancer, *Jack Hart*," Nana expressed, sitting back in her chair, sunglasses on, cold compress on her brow. "Shame you didn't take me onto the floor for a spin and a lift."

"Probably because if he tried to lift you, love, he'd break his effin' back," Gramps coughed, shovelling an entire piece of toast into his mouth. "You did right, man. Stick to dancing with your own date — if I'd have done that, I wouldn't be married to *her*."

"So, what are your plans for today, kids?" Dad asked, trying to defuse a geriatric domestic.

Jack smirked. Hopefully, he was thinking the same thing I was — wait for everyone to leave and head right back upstairs.

"We haven't really got any, Ted."

Dad rummaged in his pocket. "I'd hope you'd say that! That means you can both head into town and grab me some food before you go. The wedding absolutely cleared me out. Take the Mini, and hey — Freckles can even show you all the cool, old buildings."

I wrinkled my nose. *Don't suggest sightseeing, old man!* The last thing I wanted to do was bore Jack half to death, in a tiny car with no air con. Especially when I knew there were much better activities now available.

"We'd love to," Jack shockingly accepted, taking the keys. Was he seriously agreeing to this? Maybe he *wasn't* thinking the same as me. *Maybe he's been waiting for an excuse to forget last night, and this morning, and go back to our regular "friendship"...*

"Mel?" Jack encouraged.

I forced a fake smile, "I couldn't think of anything better."

When we eventually got into Dad's car, I drove around aimlessly.

"Are you going to be able to find your way back to the house?" Jack asked, watching another couple of signs whizz past his window. "Or are we lost?"

"We're not lost," I snapped, pulling over into the verge. "This is exactly where we're supposed to be."

Jack cranked down his window and stuck his head out. "It's a field."

I began to clamber out of the car, grabbing my bag. "Yep, we're going for a walk and a sniff. We'll find a shop eventually!"

"I thought we were going sightseeing?"

"It's a lavender field, Jack!" I snapped, starting to climb over the adjacent stone wall, "In Provence, in June. This *is* sightseeing!"

I had, in fact, got us lost. By the time we managed to find our way back to the house it was dark. Dad had dinner laid out for us on the porch. He'd usually try to go all out, as a final 'Hurrah' to our stay, but being in short supply of food, our magnificent feast consisted of tinned chicken soup, and cooked-from-frozen garlic bread.

Dad was noticeably glum as he cleared the table. I hoped it wasn't Willow's bitter toast from the other day still getting to him. I'd concluded Willow had done what she'd done at the rehearsal dinner as a way of getting back at me for bringing Jack. Rather than hurting me directly, she'd attacked the only person she knew I truly cared about. It'd almost worked too — *almost.*

Jack took a stack of bowls from Dad with a polite, "I'll do that, Ted," before carrying everything into the kitchen.

Dad watched him go with a weak, lopsided sort of smile.

"What're you thinking, Dad?" I asked, cautiously.

"Just that I'm going to miss you. It's been nice having you here this week." Dad sipped his wine, and from the way he sighed I knew there was a talk coming. "Jack seems to make you very happy."

My hands went to my hair, tucking some loose strands behind my ear. I threw a look back to the kitchen and saw Jack had started to do the washing up.

"Yeah, he does. But you say that like it's a bad thing."

Dad shrugged, then looked me right in the eye. "I just don't want to see you get hurt, love."

I laughed nervously. "What makes you think I'm going to get hurt?" I swallowed the hard lump that had appeared in my throat, tempted to pour myself another glass of wine, or just drink it straight from the bottle.

"Jack seems nice enough, Freckles. But from what I gather after everything I've read about him, and what everyone told me during the wedding, he has quite a big lifestyle back at home. I'm curious as to whether or not he has any intention of bringing you into it."

"He doesn't," I stated bluntly. "Jack and I — we're not serious, Dad."

"But you're sleeping with him—"

"Ugh," I wretched. "Please don't start making this weird. We're having a lovely evening, don't ruin it."

"I'm being serious, Mel."

"I know you are, and that's why it's weird. You don't need to worry about how serious things are with who I may or may not be sleeping with. You're my dad, you talk to me about... I don't know, but not this!"

"No," Dad pondered sorrowfully. "This was always more of your mum's domain. Boys and sex and stuff."

True, I thought. I shared almost everything with my mum. She was my go to when I was left dumped and heartbroken; or innocently confused about something sex-related. Like when Keirnan accused me of bringing a strap-on into school, and I didn't understand why everyone laughed when I thought he meant my school bag. Mum had to Google what a strap-on was when I got home. We both wished she hadn't.

"I guess I'm just concerned that, if you and Jack do decide to pursue *whatever this is—*"

"Dad, for God's sake."

He flat-out ignored me, dead set on voicing his unsolicited opinion. "I don't think you would be happy under the spotlight that he's under."

"Well, yeah..."

I'd had the smallest of tastes of Jack's limelight during my time on *Symbol of Freedom*, and that had nearly broken my confidence completely. Strangers had gotten into my head, people who didn't know a single thing about me had torn me down, stripped me bare, and made me question everything about myself. I wouldn't dream of going through that again... Let alone voluntarily.

"Maybe I'm old fashioned," Dad shrugged, sipping the last of his wine. "I think that if you're with someone, it's because you see a future with them. Or else, what are you doing, other than wasting time? I think if I learnt anything from your mum's death, it was that time isn't guaranteed, and growing old alone... is hard."

The evening has taken a very depressing turn. I had a good idea of how Jack and I would be spending our evening once we'd got dinner over and done with. But then Dad had to go and open his mouth. *Stupid, old man.* Now I'm in bed, having slipped away while Dad and Jack were talking about train lines — with *way* too much on my mind. How have I gone from having fun to overthinking everything?

Jack makes me happy, but that in itself is a very dangerous thing. In my experience, excess of happiness means heartache is not too far around the corner. The same day I had my first kiss with this boy I fancied throughout most of school, my budgie Kilo fell off his perch, dead. Similarly, the week my dad's mum died, I also won £250 on a scratch card. It was the first and only time I've ever bought a ticket. Both ends of the spectrum — the amazing and the utter shit — just seem to go hand in hand in my life.

Jack and I made a mistake. That's the conclusion I've come to. We got caught up in the moment and in a drunken second of poor judgement we threw ourselves at each other. Once we get back home, we need to give each other a stern handshake and move on with our lives. It's not like this could ever turn into anything serious... So, as Dad said, what am I doing? Other than wasting my time.

Knock. Knock. I bloody hope that's the ghost of my mum and not...

Regrettably it was Jack, he'd come to check on me.

"Mel, everything okay?" He poked his head around the bedroom door. Seeing his face brought no joy this time, just added to the pile of anxiety building in my stomach.

"Yeah," I lied. "Just a bit tired."

He entered the room hesitantly, his eyes scanning over my neatly packed suitcase. "You're eager to go home."

"Well, I didn't know what time you wanted to set off tomorrow, so I thought I'd just get my stuff together now."

"Okay," Jack perched on the edge of my bed. He frowned when he noticed my knees were pulled up to my chest with my arms wrapped around them. "What's wrong?"

"Nothing. I told you, I'm just tired."

"Tired Mel sits in sweatpants with a brew. Sad Mel wallows in the dark."

"I'm not wallowing."

"You've been off since dinner."

"The soup gave me an iffy tummy," I shrugged, straightening out my legs, tempted to crawl under the covers and just cry. I didn't need Jack in my room, acting all supportive and caring. I needed him to go back to being an arrogant arsehole so that I could end this for a better reason than: *I don't want to waste my time shagging you in case I wind up with cancer like my mum and die before I'm 50.* Or, *I'd like to not grow old on my own like my dad, so maybe I should stop shagging you and focus more of my time on someone who I actually see a future with.*

"I swear, I'm fine."

Jack placed his hand on my calf. My ears immediately went hot, my stomach twisting. He gingerly moved his hand further up my leg. He crawled up the bed, his fingers lingering between my thighs, "You're a really terrible liar, Mel."

My breath caught silently in my chest as I felt him grow hard. "That's quite disheartening considering I'm an actor."

Jack chuckled, pushing his whole weight into me. In a split-second it turned from sexy to suffocating. With him on top of me, I suddenly couldn't breathe.

"Stop."

Jack didn't need telling twice. He sat up briskly, his hands raised, surrendering, eyes wide with panic. "Everything okay?"

"Yeah, I just—" I sat upright, my chest incredibly tight. "I can't breathe."

Jack hopped off the bed, heading straight for the balcony doors. Opening them welcomed in a cool breeze and a symphony of crickets.

"You want some water?" Jack was already heading for the bathroom before I could reply, returning with a small glass and holding it out to me. "That any better?"

"Yeah, fine, thanks. Just sit down before you pull something."

I took the glass and placed it on the bedside table, Jack awkwardly sitting on the bed as far away from me as possible.

The crickets didn't help the uncomfortable silence.

"Okay, I've clearly missed something. Like, do I grab my shovel now and start guessing what I've done wrong? Or are you going to save us both some time and just come right out and tell me?"

I rolled my eyes, "Oh, I'm sorry, Jack, I didn't realise you had somewhere to be right now."

"*Jesus,* Mel, what is wrong with you?" Jack stood up. I'd hoped that meant he was leaving, but no. "Have I said something? Done something?"

I pulled my hair out of its bun and scrunched my bobble in my fists. "You haven't done anything, Jack. I'm just tired, and would prefer to be left alone!"

"Okay," Jack stormed off towards the door. "I really like you, Mel," he snapped, turning back to me. "As a friend. I think you're thoughtful, and cool. I think you're talented and funny. But dear God, as a person? You're tapped in the head. You don't know whether you're coming or going, whether you're into me or not. I've been clear with you from the start—"

"Yeah, you have. You've told me about the PR relationships, and made it clear you were going to be my fake boyfriend this week. But everyone's gone now, Jack. You can stop pretending, and we can just go back to being mates. It's what's best — stops us both from wasting our time, thinking this is something that it's not."

Jack took a beat before nodding, his shoulders tense as he reached for the door handle. "Okay. Glad that's all been cleared up then."

He slammed the door behind himself and the room went still. I heard his feet pound down the hallway. His own bedroom door slammed, and then silence.

I couldn't help but grab my pillow and scream into it. That wasn't the way I saw things ending but I can't complain when it's what I wanted.

That's a lie. I didn't want any of this. I wanted Jack next to me, holding me close and kissing me all over. Why had I done this again? Oh, yeah, because of one stupid comment my dad had made that I'd let get into my head. I couldn't just enjoy myself, could I? Couldn't just take Jack while I had him, and dealt with all this when we got home and it no doubt ended naturally. God, why am I like this?

It's true what they say — never get romantically involved with an actor.

13th June

Seriously considering writing a book called, 'How to Procrastinate'.
Just three words — 'To write, later'.

It's confirmed. Jack and I are as stubborn as each other. We spent the entire morning in silence, right up until the moment we were sat next to each other on the plane, both of us refusing to be the first one to speak.

The atmosphere in the car on the way to the airport hadn't exactly been pleasant. Dad had driven, dropped us off, given me a squeeze and Jack a 'Hope to see you again soon,' with a brisk handshake.

Jack's response: 'We'll see'.

I could've died.

"We sure picked the right day to head home," Jack mused, finally cracking. He peered out of his droplet-stained window at the fields below. "Not like British rain though, is it? When it rains abroad it's swelteringly hot, British rain is cold and miserable."

I gripped tighter onto the book I was pretending to read. These were the first words he'd said to me all day.

"You're *seriously* choosing to talk about the weather?" I scoffed, rolling my eyes without even realising. "God, we have sex once—"

"Three times, actually."

"Have one heated conversation—"

"*Argument,*" Jack clarified.

"And now we're left talking about the bloody weather? I should have just kept my legs shut and stuck with the better conversation."

Jack chuckled, his cheeks noticeably a little flushed, his voice low. "Alright, I'm unsure of what to say right now, so sue me."

"Don't tempt me, Jack. I know what your net worth is."

"What do *you* want to talk about then? Because clearly I can't say anything at the moment without it turning into a *heated conversation*."

I sighed, unable to stop myself from smiling. Even when uptight, Jack was still a charming sod.

"Fine," I resigned. "What're you up to next week?"

"Why? Are you planning a surprise for me?"

"*No*. I just know you have a busy schedule. To be honest, I was surprised you had a week free at all. Half expected your agent to call and whisk you away at the last minute."

Jack shrugged, looking out the window. "Michael did call, I just ignored him."

My jaw dropped slightly. "What do you mean, Michael called?"

Jack's attention turned back to me, "I mean that Michael, my agent, called me a few times this week for various stuff, but I told him I was busy. I don't know how to make that any clearer, Mel."

"Why would you do that?"

A line had appeared between Jack's eyebrows, his lips thin. "Do you really think that badly of me? You think I'd jump ship on a promise I made to you because of a job offer, or whatever is on the table?"

I thought back to the countless times I'd deserted my dad for an audition. Jumped on a plane, waved him goodbye and run home selfishly, without a second thought.

"I just know work commitments can get in the way of things," I said, ignoring the bile that was creeping up my throat.

"I have a few meetings next week," Jack eventually said. "And an interview with some foreign magazine at some point, but that hasn't been finalised. And you know, going to see my grandad. Does that answer your question?"

"Sure," I forced a smile and turned a page. *Stopped paying attention about six pages ago, but hey-ho.* "So I guess you'll be pretty busy then?"

"I guess."

Jack knew just how to make my brain itch. I'd realised he wasn't one for giving straight-forward answers unless food or sex was involved. Anything else, I get some crappy-flappy answer that sends my brain spinning.

We went back to silence. The book wasn't working. I thought maybe putting some headphones in would reassure Jack he didn't have to make conversation, but as I reached for my bag—

"What about you? What are your plans when you get back?"

"Well..." *Sarcastic mode: activated*, "I have my *beautiful* apron and name tag waiting for me back at the café, not to mention double shifts to make up for missing an entire week. It's going to be gruelling stuff, but you know what, I can hardly wait."

Jack laughed and I found myself laughing along with him. The air actually felt a little thinner, the atmosphere much more bearable.

"That sounds pretty crap," Jack placed his hand on my thigh. "I'm sorry."

I tried to ignore the tingling sensation his touch was sending up my leg. "S'okay. I mean, it's not all bad. I get to wear these *really* hot plimsolls that I can honestly say are the sexiest thing I own."

"Might need to judge that for myself."

Jack moved his hand from my thigh to the back of my neck and suddenly my whole body had grown hot. How had we gone from barely speaking to potentially becoming members of the mile-high club. *I'm sure Jack already is a member, to be fair.*

"You've got that look on your face," Jack smirked. "Does that mean I'm out of the doghouse?"

I opened my book again, trying to keep my trembling hands busy. *Any random page will do.*

"Mel," Jack whispered in my ear, "we both know you're not reading that book."

Jack's fingers began to wrap themselves up in the loose strands from my bun. He tugged on them playfully, planting a kiss on my bare shoulder.

"I know I said I'd drop you off at home, but I'm thinking it'd be really good if you came back to mine."

Jesus.

"So, what do you say?"

I cleared my throat. "I don't think me participating in the game you're playing is a good idea, Jack," I breathed, amazed I'd managed to construct an entire sentence.

"Who says I'm playing a game?" Jack muttered, pressing his soft lips to my neck. "Answer the damn question, Mel. Do you want to come back to mine, or not?"

I began screaming at myself: *Say something clever! Make good choices.*

"Yeah, sounds good."

You idiot.

No coherent thought had been able to manifest itself the entire journey home. The suspense was going to kill me.

"This is us," Jack said, pulling up onto the pavement.

I imagined Jack's house to be one of those million-dollar mansions you saw on the music channel as a kid. I don't know why. I thought he'd have six bright yellow sports cars on the drive, an indoor cinema, a pool. But he didn't. It was just some regular, red-brick townhouse, with a glossy white front door.

My stomach had suddenly gotten very heavy. This was definitely not the brightest idea I'd ever had. But then I felt Jack's hand on my thigh again. His touch brought on a gentle wave of calm.

"Come on."

Before I could protest, Jack was lifting both cases out of the boot.

"You can just leave my bag in the car," I found myself saying, not realising how whorey it sounded. *I'm only coming in for a shag.* Thankfully, Jack hadn't heard. He was too busy fighting with the front door. He finally managed to open it.

"Temperamental door?" I teased, nervously stepping past him and over the threshold.

"No, it's just got a bit of an attitude." He dropped the cases in the hall and before I knew it, I'd jumped him.

My body, in sheer panic knowing this was the last time I would sleep with (and probably see) Jack, had thrown itself at him before the door had even been shut. Jack took care of that with a swift kick, his desperate moan vibrating against my lips.

"God, I thought *I* was keen," he laughed, pushing me against the wall.

"I'm not keen," I breathed. "Just all that door talk really got me going."

"I'll keep that in mind for later," Jack panted, grabbing my thighs and wrapping my legs around his waist. "That was the *longest* drive of my life," he groaned as I kissed up and down his (not-yet recovered) neck.

"Should have just pulled over and taken me on the back seat."

Jack went still, his fists scrunching up my top. "You could have told me that was an option."

I pressed my forehead against his, laughing softly. "Sorry."

Jack's brooding pout was adorably sexy.

I entangled my fingers in his hair, pulling on the strands.

"Where's your bedroom?" I gasped, my toes curling. Since this was going to be the last time Jack saw me, I wanted him to remember it.

"Up the stairs, second door on the right. *Why*?"

I wriggled out from under him. As soon as his hands fell from my waist, I pulled my top up and over my head. After unclipping my bra and pulling down my jeans, I dropped everything I had been wearing onto the floor. Jack looked as though he might eat me alive. *Perfect.*

"Up the stairs and second door on the right, wasn't it?"

Jack gulped, his eyes fixed on my naked body. "*Jesus,* and here I was thinking we were just going to do it up against the wall..."

"I'm sure your bedroom has walls, Jack."

Jack re-entered his bedroom with his dressing gown open, his boxers exposed, and a steaming mug of tea in each hand.

"Milk, two sugars," he passed me the purple mug, and placed his red one on top of the dresser.

I couldn't help but throw a glance at the bedside clock. *Nearly six*. Ian had been expecting me home around two.

"It's getting late."

Jack chuckled, laying beside me on the bed. "Should I expect you to turn into a pumpkin?"

"No, just thinking about heading home," I cleared my throat, Jack's stare a little unsettling. "You know, Ian will be wondering where I am. Not to mention I'm getting kind of hungry."

"Oh," Jack shrugged, resting his head back against the headboard. "Well, you can always eat here before you go. I don't really have any food in, but I could order us a takeaway. What're you in the mood for?"

He reached for his phone.

"What about Ian?"

"Is he joining us?"

"No, I just mean — what do I tell him?"

Jack frowned. "What do you want to tell him?"

I felt that bile in my throat again. No point telling Ian about something that was basically over. "I'll tell him our flight got delayed."

I shuffled out from under the covers and pulled Jack's discarded shirt on.

"Fancy a Chinese takeaway?" he asked just as I was leaving the room to find my phone.

I popped my head back around the doorframe and laughed. "Order me crispy chilli beef and I'll never leave."

"Good to know."

Ian's voice was high, panicked. "Where are you? Jack was supposed to be dropping you off like *four hours ago!*"

"Calm down," I hissed, sitting beside my suitcase in the hallway. "Our flight got delayed, we're still in France."

"Oh my God, by four hours? What the hell happened?"

"Err…" I blanked, distracted by my pile of discarded clothes. "Something wrong with the engine?" I bit my lip as the line suddenly went silent.

"*The engine*? Mel," Ian breathed deeply, excitement in his voice already building, "where *are* you?"

"*Ian—*" I warned, but it was no use. Ian had begun hollering down the phone.

"Oh my God. You're at Jack Hart's aren't you? Are you shagging? I *knew* it! I can honestly say I've never been prouder."

"Ian," I repeated when he took a pause for breath. "Jack and I are just friends, okay? Nothing to be proud of. We're just chilling at his."

"Chilling? That's code for banging the living daylights out of each other!"

"I will be home later, *okay*? That's all I was calling to tell you, because that is all there is to know."

"I don't believe you," Ian laughed maniacally. "I *cannot* wait to see Tilly's face when I tell her! She'll combust, I swear."

"Ian," my voice went rigid with stress, "for God's sake, you're not saying anything to Tilly. Or Amarra. Or your mum. Or your coke-sniffing date, okay? Because there is *nothing to say*. I'll be home in a couple of hours — try not to ruin my life in the meantime."

I heard Ian choke on his own laughter and decided I was fighting a lost cause. I hung up and preemptively cringed at the thought of having to explain this to Jack.

He found me sitting at the round, marble breakfast table in the kitchen, playing idly with my phone.

"Ian know you're alive?"

"Mmm... and here. So if paparazzi show up on the doorstep, you know who's blabbed," I joked, trying to avoid Jack's wandering gaze.

"And you told Ian you were here *because...?*"

My stomach churned as I got a sudden suspicion that my dinner was about to get cancelled. "I'm a terrible liar?"

"Well, I already knew that," Jack chuckled, placing his empty mug in the dishwasher. "Crispy chilli beef is on its way. Ordered some lemon chicken, spring rolls, egg fried rice and some prawn toast as well."

"Wow, guess I wasn't the only one getting hungry."

"Worked up quite an appetite," Jack wriggled his eyebrows. "So we'll eat, and then you wanted to head home, yeah?"

Head home — it was nice to know Jack and I were on the same page. We were ending this with a bang, *literally*. I forced a smile and looked at my silly reflection in the harrowing black screen of my phone.

"Yeah."

14th June

Your own mind is your own worst enemy.

Ian had waited up. I'd found him like some uptight mother waiting in the front room. I didn't say a word. Didn't know what to say. Jack had dropped me off, given me my case with a quick kiss on the cheek, and that was it. That was the end of it. I knew it was going to happen, but it still hurt.

A hangover-like migraine hit me like a tonne of bricks almost as soon as I got through the front door. Ian called it 'orgasm exhaustion'.

Through a haze of black spots, I'd managed to find a flannel and douse it in cold water.

"So, when are you seeing Jack again?" Ian asked giddily from behind the bathroom door. "Tomorrow? This weekend?"

"I'm not." I placed the flannel across my forehead, slumping to the floor with my back against the bath.

"Because you have a headache? Or because you need a couple of days for the friction burn to cool off?"

If I could have rolled my eyes without it feeling like my skull was going to implode, I would've.

"*Because* I won't be seeing Jack again."

"I don't understand," he squeaked, the door flying open and hitting the wall. A thunder clap went off in my head. I could've been sick. "What do you mean you won't be seeing Jack again? You have to! I need you too!" Ian was gripping his phone so tightly it looked like it might break in his hand. "You can't fuck and chuck someone like *Jack Hart!*"

"Ian, how many times do I have to tell you?" I felt my whole body melting into the water-stained floor tiles, "Jack took me to my cousin's wedding as a favour, and then we ate Chinese food at his house. That's it."

"So you *haven't* shagged him?"

I tried to push aside the memory of Jack bearing down on me. "I have not—" an echo of one of his moans reverberated in my ear, "—had sex with Jack Hart."

Amarra was harder to convince. My migraine was still in full force when she showed up with a bottle of wine and a family-sized packet of cheese puffs. She drank the wine, I ate the cheese puffs. She'd been smart enough to wait until Ian had reluctantly left for work, to make sure she could really give herself the best chance of getting the truth out of me. Eventually I caved. I told her everything. The kiss Jack and I shared in Manchester. The kiss we'd had at wrap, everything that happened while we were in France, and every little detail of what had transpired when we got back.

Amarra sipped some more of her wine and nibbled on a cheese puff, my quilt up to her chin, the movie playing on my laptop long forgotten.

"Okay, so you fucked it."

"What?" I scoffed. "What do you mean?"

She shrugged, not shying away from hurting my feelings. "It sounds like you have properly gone and shafted yourself, babe. The guy's into you! Or at least he *was,* he might not be now you've given him the brush off."

"You're mad— Jack has never been into me."

Amarra rolled her eyes, "My God, girl, you snogged in Manchester and then *you* ran off. He didn't remind you of it when you said you were too drunk to recall what had happened because maybe he was fearful of being rejected by sober you."

"Give over…"

"And then he kisses you at wrap. Now this one's weird, but you did look banging to be fair, for which I take full credit."

"Well, of course you would."

"Thank you. So, you look amazing, he tells you that and then he kisses you. Fair. Then you, technically — well, half-jokingly — invite him to Willow's wedding, and he accepts. Now, yeah, most people would jump at the chance of a free holiday, but I think it went deeper than that. I think he liked you, but you've basically got back and thrown him away. And if a guy did that to me, especially if we hooked up, yeah, I'd cut and run. Not worth it."

"But I'm sure he was the one who—"

"Babe, are you that blind? You're the one who's called quits on this without even asking him where he sees it going! You're the one who wanted to come home last night instead of staying with him. From the sounds of it, Jack would've kept bonking you for a few more days, if not for the rest of his life."

"Because it's bonking innit, not because he likes me!"

"He literally said he liked you! Those exact words, Mel."

"He meant as a friend—"

Amarra pulled a face, "Seriously, do you hear yourself?"

"Okay, even if Jack really did like me, and wanted to make something of us, we still wouldn't work. You know that. I know that. Jack knows that. So I did the right thing ending it with him before it even started. *I did.*"

"Right," Amarra drained her wine, "you keep telling yourself that."

I've done nothing but stare at my ceiling since Amarra left. *Is that mould coming through the wall?* Now is not the time to be thinking about the poorly plastered walls of my room.

Amarra has set my mind spiralling and now I can't help but go over every little detail regarding Jack. I like Jack, I really do, but me as his girlfriend? It's almost laughable. I'd have to deal with everything I went through during *Symbol* — and I bet that wasn't even a real taste of it. I bet if I was Jack's girlfriend I'd have to cope with so much more. Hate from his fans hitting me from every angle, for every second of the day. Paparazzi outside my front door. My own identity would go straight down the toilet as I'd only be known as *Jack Hart's Girlfriend* and nothing more. My acting career would be jeopardised. My privacy—

What am I rambling about?

This is beyond ridiculous, farcical even. Jack doesn't even like me.

God, I'm starting to agree with Amarra... I may have well and truly messed this up.

Bollocks.

20th June

I think losing my teeth is my biggest fear, to be honest. That and being skinned alive.

Amarra was full on coaching me throughout the entire retrieval process. We had decided to wait a week so as not to come across too desperate. I would wait seven days, then if Jack made any form of contact — great, I would reply. But otherwise, I had to wait a full seven days.

"But if he already thinks I'm not into him then surely I should tell him I am into him as soon as possible?"

"No," Amarra insisted, "let him sweat! Let him yearn, and then when you do come crawling back, he'll be even more grateful, and even more obsessed with you than before, for the fear he may lose you again!"

Why are we like this? Why are we, as a generation, as a human race, like this? What was wrong with telling someone you liked them because you liked them, and breaking up with them because you no longer did? What happened to courting? To falling in love? To being open and honest about your feelings and just saying what was on your mind?

We're on day six. Jack has made zero contact. Not one random text, so my confidence in Amarra's plan is waning.

My phone is just lying there on the bedside. I can see it. All it would take is one call. One call, to straighten this misunderstanding out and throw myself back into Jack's (hopefully) welcoming arms.

Sod it.

I'm ringing him.

There was no answer. So, regrettably, I tried again, and I hate to admit it but he now has about twenty-six missed calls from me. Maybe he'll find it endearing? Or he'll think it's an emergency and ring me as soon as he sees? Or maybe he'll think I'm crazy and block my number.

What have I done? I need to fix this, and *fast*.

I might have lost it but I was past caring. Amarra begged me not to if I wanted to salvage any chance I had with Jack, but I'd made up my mind. I wasn't listening to her anymore. I was going round to his house.

"You can't just show up at his door!" Amarra screamed at me down the phone. "You're going to scare him off! Seriously, get back on the tube and go home. Take a cold shower and — just like, handcuff yourself to the radiator. Please, don't do this!"

"I'll tell him I left something at his house and I came over to pick it up."

"That's going to fall through when he sees you pick up *nothing*!"

I turned the corner and saw Jack's front door come into view.

"Well, I'm here now, so—"

I hung up and, without thinking, pressed the doorbell.

I waited.

There was no answer.

I rung again.

And waited.

Still no answer.

Then the doubt started to sink in. *Where did he say he was going to be this week?* I went to ring again when the door finally opened. It was a woman, with sharp features, slicked-back red hair and eyelashes as long as my forearm. "Hello...?" she asked, nervously.

I took a step back and double-checked the outside of the house. *This was Jack's house, right?* I blinked at her and tried to ignore the heavy weight growing in my stomach.

"Is Jack in?"

"Hold on, just give me two secs," she closed the door in my face and I honestly felt like bolting. Why the hell was there another woman in Jack's house? Was this his next victim? His next co-star? A desperate woman, just like me, who'd fallen for his charms and bullshit?

The woman finally reappeared with a phone to her ear. "Yeah, she's right here. What's your name?"

I blinked. "Mel—"

"She says her name's Mel. Do you know a Mel?"

Does he know a Mel? Inside, I was screaming. *He'd better fucking say, 'Yes'.*

The woman suddenly offered her phone out to me. "He wants to speak to you," she encouraged me to take it, but I'd suddenly lost all confidence. He had another woman in his house, that clearly meant whatever had occurred between us was well and truly over. I'd blown it.

I reluctantly took her phone and held it to my ear. Immediately, I could hear Jack's heavy breathing.

"Hello...?"

"Mel? Are you okay?"

Not really, no. I thought. "Yeah, fine," I lied. "Where are you?"

Jack sniffed. "I'm on my way to the hospital."

My stomach dropped. "Oh my God, are you okay?"

"Yeah," he quickly reassured, "I'm just visiting my grandad." I heard him laugh nervously. "It's been a week or so, so I'm a bit nervous to see the state he's gotten himself into, to be honest."

I looked back at the redhead who was leaning against Jack's front door, arms folded against her chest, waiting not so patiently for her phone back.

"Well, do you want me to meet you? I can come to the hospital if you need someone there with you?" Part of me wondered why I'd offered. Surely the woman in his house should be the one there supporting him.

"Oh," Jack hesitated, "Yeah, that'd be great."

God, I hate hospitals. The last time I was in a hospital, my mum was going through some severe medication withdrawal. I saw four nurses pin her down to stop herself from ripping all the tubes out of her arm and smacking the crap out of the doctor. Dad and I had been brought in to try and calm her but it had gotten to a point where she didn't know who we were, and she needed sedating.

I stood beside my traumatised dad as we watched her wail and kick with everything she had.

"They're trying to kill me!" she screamed at the top of her lungs. "They're trying to kill me!"

Through the bars of her hospital bed I could see her bloodshot eyes were fixed on me.

"Mum, they're trying to help you—"

Her neck suddenly craned back, her body contorting itself, desperate to break free.

Dad's hands flew to his ears, Mum's screams becoming unbearable the moment the doctor's needles pierced her skin. I thought I was going to throw up when she suddenly jerked against the bars and smacked her face. Blood started flowing freely from her nose, her whole body trembling, losing the fight to whatever sedation was now coursing through her.

"They're trying to kill me," she repeated, her voice now weak. "I don't want to die..."

Like I said, *I hate hospitals.*

Jack met me at reception, his eyes puffy and sore. As soon as he saw me, he immediately pulled me into a tight hug and buried his face into the nape of my neck.

"I brought you a coffee," I said, holding it over his shoulder, grateful he hadn't spilled it on either of us.

"Oh, thank you," he pulled away and took the coffee. "Hospital coffee always tastes like piss."

"I know… How're you holding up?" I asked, as that always seemed to be the go-to question people would ask me when Mum was sick.

"I've been better," Jack shook his head. "Thought Grandad may have had some visitors while I've been away, but no one has been to see him. Like, my mum hasn't even rung him. Said she's too busy doing absolutely sod all. Like *Jesus,* her dad's dying and she can't even take a break from being herself to be there for him, you know?"

I grabbed Jack's free hand and squeezed it, knowing there was nothing I could say to help. So, I did what I always wished more people had done for me, and said nothing at all.

Jack's grandad looked like a well-groomed, shorter and thinner version of Santa Claus. His face was embedded with countless laughter lines. As we entered the room, his eyes creased further at the corners, suddenly full of wonder and joy. Two clear tubes hung loosely out of his nostrils, resting on his bright white moustache.

"Jack, you found Josie!"

Jack gripped my hand tightly and choked on his own breath. "No, sorry, Grandad. Mum isn't here yet, this is my friend, Melissa. Mel, this is my grandad, Arthur."

I sat by his bedside and smiled as confidently as I could. "Nice to meet you, Sir."

"*Sir*!" Arthur breathed, smiling widely. "She can stay."

A nurse popped her head in through the door and acknowledged me briefly, before asking Jack if she could have a quick word outside in the corridor. Jack nervously agreed and left the room. "I'll be right back," he reassured me.

"So, what do you do, Melissa?" Arthur asked weakly after a moment's silence.

I no longer really knew how to answer that question. I couldn't really call myself an actor when I seemed to do everything *but* acting work. However, with zero auditions and no opportunities lined up, *Symbol of Freedom* was yet to be released, so I supposed, technically, I could still consider myself *an actor*.

"I'm an actor," I said, feeling like a liar as the words were coming out of my mouth.

"Oh, like Jack?"

I couldn't help but smile. Arthur said Jack's name with such pride and joy in his face. There was real love there.

"Yeah, sort of like Jack. Though he's a lot busier than me."

"He's very good," Arthur smiled even wider, taking sharp breaths between his words. "He's on the telly. Though I wish he'd do more theatre, no one seems to want to do theatre anymore."

I did a double-take, thinking *maybe Jack wanting to do more theatre wasn't about reconnecting with his craft after all?*

"Do you like theatre, Arthur?"

He wriggled into his hospital bedding. "Oh, I love it."

"Me too."

Arthur raised his bushy white eyebrows, "Do you do theatre?"

"No, I don't," I replied. "I think I'd like to write for the theatre though."

"Mmm..." Arthur inhaled deeply, pushing his tubes further into his nose with the back of his hand. "You can make a lot of difference with a good play."

"Yeah, you can," I agreed.

"Jack needs to do more theatre," Arthur repeated. "He's an actor, you know?"

I forced an uncomfortable smile. This was all too familiar. The image of my mum crept to the front of my mind. She had become like this, lying in her hospital bed, stuffed to her eyeballs with medication. Short-term memory well and truly shot. Looping a conversation like a broken record. I did what I'd learnt to do with her and played along as best I could.

"Is he?" I replied.

Arthur nodded, his eyes lighting up with the same pride and joy as before. "He's on the telly. What do you do?"

"I—"

Arthur reached out and touched my hand affectionately, not waiting for my answer. "Do you know when Josie will be here?"

I felt a swell in my chest. I assumed Josie was Jack's mum.

Arthur looked at me expectantly for an answer that I didn't have. Thankfully, as I choked, a woman came into the room with a sheet of paper in her hand.

"Oh good, you're still here. Sorry to interrupt, Mr West, but I've got something for your visitor, if that's okay?"

"Fine by me," Arthur smiled, his laughter lines reappearing.

The nurse passed me the paper. "I just need you to fill this in for me, please."

I looked at it, confused and slightly thrown. It must have been some visitor's information thing. It asked for my name and contact information. Probably something they do in case of a fire alarm to make sure they have a log of everyone that has come in and out of the building.

I filled it in and passed it back to her. Arthur was now staring at me, his eyes filled with nothing but love. As the woman left, he leaned into me, retaking my hand, and whispering, "You look like my Josie."

I look like Jack's mum? That's not weird at all.

"But she's got white hair, not red like you."

That makes it a bit better, I guess.

"Is Josie here yet?" Arthur asked Jack when he came back into the room, not yet letting go of my hand.

Jack hesitated. "No, Grandad, she's not here yet."

A little spark of joy evaporated from Arthur's face. Jack tried to hide his own disappointment with a forced grin. "But the nurses say you can be discharged tomorrow. They're going to send you home with some oxygen for when you need it, and we've set up a care plan. You'll get to be back in your own bed. That's something, isn't it?"

Arthur nodded, "Good. Thank you, Jack."

"So, I'll come back tomorrow with the car, and I'll take you home, okay?"

Arthur squeezed my hand as best he could. "Will you be bringing your friend?"

Jack shook his head, without even looking at me, "No, Grandad. I don't think so."

Well, that answers that, I thought.

We stayed for a little while but I could see Jack getting more uncomfortable with every repeated conversation or mention of Josie. As we left the room, a huge weight seemed to lift off his shoulders. He breathed deeply and took my hand, before gingerly kissing my cheek.

"Thank you for that," he whispered, leading me back the way we had come in.

"No problem."

Without discussing it, we went outside and leisurely strolled towards the tube station. The conversation was unbearably minimal. A few questions about my week, a few about his. They couldn't have been more polar opposite. I'd been waitressing, and essentially doing nothing but gawking over my phone for six days. Jack had been to a couple of auditions and several meetings for the up-and-coming press tour for *Violins in Vienna*'s next season. No wonder he'd made no attempt to get in touch, he hadn't had the time.

As we approached his house, I could see the red-haired woman locking up. Jack began to break into a jog, leaving me in his wake.

If she starts to run towards him, and an orchestra starts to play, I'm going to unalive myself.

She didn't. Thank God.

She seemed frustrated with him more than anything else.

"Don't bother locking the door, Jess," Jack waved, "saves me having to fight it open again."

"Okay," she replied, removing her key from the door, "I was having a hard time myself."

I looked over Jack's shoulder at *Jess*. She was pretty. Prettier than me, that's for sure.

"You found him then?" She joked, uncomfortable.

"Yeah," I clearly wasn't the only one noticing the awkward tension building between the three of us.

Jack cleared his throat. "Right, I'll see you at the same time next week."

Jess nodded, "Yeah, sounds good."

I followed Jack into the house as Jess walked off down the street. I was both eager to learn and terrified of the answer, so found myself asking, "Who's Jess?" the moment the door had closed behind us.

"She's my cleaner."

Ah. I mentally smacked myself round the face. *You idiot.*

Jack was smirking. Clearly, he'd read my mind again and knew what I'd been thinking. I couldn't hide the fact I was relieved. More than relieved — I was thrilled. Jack hadn't moved on. He hadn't got another woman in his house. He hadn't completely forgotten all about me.

Jack sniffed his collar and grimaced. "God, I need a shower, I stink of hospital." He removed his coat and threw it on the bannister, "Do you want a brew?"

Not really, I thought. Now that my brain had settled from the whole Jess situation, I felt a bit more inclined to actually have a proper conversation.

"The reason I came over this morning..." I began.

"Milk, two sugars?" Jack ignored me, making his way to the kitchen.

"Jack, I just wanted to apologise," I persisted, scuttling after him. "I think I got a bit ahead of myself after we got back, and I was wondering if—"

"Big mug or little mug?" Jack opened the cupboard and flicked the kettle on.

"I really thought you just wanted a bit of fun," I persisted. I wasn't going to let my overthinking get on top of me this time. "No matter what you said, I guess I just didn't really hear any of it. And I'm sorry if I hurt you, or gave you the wrong idea about my feelings. I do like you, Jack — like, really *really* like you — and I'd really like it if we could maybe go on a proper date?"

Jack groaned loudly, "Oh God, Mel..." The kettle started to boil. "I'm not being funny, but this is so not what I need right now," he swallowed hard, and I felt my entire heart drop into my stomach.

"Okay..."

He buried his head in his hands, never looking up at me. "Don't get me wrong, it's nice hearing you say all this stuff, it's stuff I've been wanting to hear for weeks, but I can't be doing with this. Not today. Not right now."

"I'm sorry, I—"

"I've got Michael up my arse, with zero empathy for what I'm going through, using contract jargon to dictate my every move. I'm flying to Brazil later this week for God-knows how long, with no idea if my grandad is going to kick the bucket while I'm over there." Jack laughed, manically. "And if he does die while I'm out there, he's going to be completely on his own because my mum can't be arsed to be a decent human being for once in her life!" Jack snapped and I watched as his entire body tensed. "I just — I can't deal with you along with everything else right now. Does that make sense?"

A million questions began to shoot off like fireworks in my head. The biggest, and loudest of them all: *Would he have felt this way if I had told him how I felt sooner?* It wasn't the time to ask that. And it wouldn't have helped, whatever his answer.

"Yes," I eventually replied, "That makes sense."

Jack finally looked up at me, his face unreadable. "Thank you for understanding."

Thank you for letting me down easy, I thought.

The kettle finished boiling.

"Now, do you want a brew before you go, or not?"

30th June

One of Mum's most memorable phrases was 'Ignore the why'. If we start asking ourselves why certain things happen, especially the traumatic things, we will begin to lose ourselves very quickly.

I found myself reflecting on the subject of 'rejection' today. I've concluded that it sucks. Doesn't matter if it's in your personal or professional life. It just sucks.

You're not wanted. Plain and simple. That's all there is to it.

While I was lost in thought, I received a *ping* on my email. An audition. I almost couldn't believe it, unable to recall how long it had been since the last one. A month? Maybe two? According to Bethany, the industry had been 'quiet' — more like dead *silent*.

I glanced over the breakdown — a small part in a horror movie. *Really?* I hated horror films. Never understood the appeal. It's either slashing, stabbing, or screaming.

I immediately rang Bethany, who left me waiting until the voicemail was a second away.

"Good Morning, Bethany Rollins speaking. Can I ask who's calling?"

"Hi, Bethany, it's Melissa."

"Oh, hiya, love. Is everything okay?"

"Yeah, I'm just ringing about that email you just sent through. The audition for *Blood and Gory*? I think I'm going to pass on it."

There was a moment's silence that felt like an eternity.

"What do you mean? Mel, you've never passed on an audition. Is everything okay?"

"I just don't think it's a good use of my time."

"Oh," Bethany stalled. "Are you busy? Do you need me to contact casting and rearrange your audition slot?"

"No, I'm just saying that I don't want to do it. I don't see myself doing the job, if by some chance I got an offer for it. So there's really no point in me doing the audition... Is that okay?" I had a strong feeling it wasn't from the second I asked.

Bethany inhaled deeply. "I think, at this moment in time, before *Symbol of Freedom* comes out, you should really be making use of these meetings, Melissa. Even if it's just about seeing the casting director and building up a good rapport with them."

"The casting directors are never in the room for parts this small, Bethany. You know that. I'll just end up seeing an assistant who also knows this part isn't for me. So can I just not do it, *please*?"

Another moment's silence that felt even longer than eternity.

"Okay, fine. I'll let casting know."

"Thanks Bethany, I really app—"

The line went dead.

I knew in my heart of hearts that I should've cared about the fact Bethany had hung up on me without so much as a goodbye but, in all honesty, I didn't. I was relieved I didn't have to go to an audition for a job I didn't want. *Or maybe*, I wondered, *I'm just glad not to be going to an audition at all.*

No audition meant one less opportunity of being rejected. It had been nearly two weeks since Jack's brush off and yet it still weighed heavy on my mind. Industry rejection on top of that? *No, thank you.*

I realised I had well and truly become exhausted with the entire thing. *Symbol of Freedom* aside — and that was just a fluke — what had I actually done with my acting career since I started? If you could even call it a career. I'd done small parts in TV shows, and even they'd been cut down to barely a second of screen time. I'd done bits and pieces, one-offs and walk-ons, and that was it. That was really *it*. Why had I been chasing this for so long? Why had I been holding a terrible set of cards this whole time, adamant that it was a winning hand?

Maybe I had been so desperate to be successful as an actor because it meant I never had to be myself. And by never being myself I would never have to look at my reflection in the mirror and acknowledge there was a motherless, frightened little girl staring back at me. Maybe it was finally time to find out who she was, what she wanted. And maybe, *just maybe,* find a way to help her to let go.

"I think that if you're with someone it's because you see a future with them. Or else, what are you doing, other than wasting time?"

If I applied my dad's words to my career then I really was wasting time. I couldn't see a future in this industry. Not anymore. I couldn't see myself still dragging my sorry arse to pointless auditions for the rest of my life. I couldn't see myself still trying to be a successful actor at fifty... *If I even make it to fifty.*

"I think if I learnt anything from your mum's death, it's that time isn't guaranteed—"

I quickly opened up a blank document on my laptop. The page was intimidating, but somehow words were finding their way to the surface. Before I knew it, I was typing.

Waiting for Monday

Elle enters stage right: [with a chair in hand. She places it facing the audience and sits].

ELLE: 'I'm not a good person', I confess to my mum, who no longer has the strength to lift up her head. She smiles softly at me. 'I don't think anyone is,' she says, 'not really.' The doctors said she had three to twelve months left to live. We got 9 weeks.

It wasn't until Ian poked his head round my bedroom door and asked what I wanted for dinner that I realised how late it'd gotten. My eyes hurt, straining in the dark, staring at a brightly-lit screen on a laptop with almost 0% battery.

"What're you doing?" Ian asked, flicking on the big light and almost blinding me.

"Nothing," I shut my laptop and plugged it in to charge.

"Have you heard from ya boyfriend today?" Ian smirked, pointing at my phone. I'd decided to fill Ian in on *some* of the details regarding Jack, but not all. He hounded me for three days straight when pictures of me leaving Jack's house had appeared online. Our relationship was well and truly a work of fiction for all of Jack's fan base to scrutinise. It had very much cemented in my mind that, yes, I wasn't fit for that kind of attention and maybe Jack rejecting me had been the best outcome for us both. Amarra called it 'dodging a bullet'.

I'd told Ian that Jack and I definitely weren't dating, and to a point weren't even on speaking terms anymore as I hadn't heard from since he left for his press tour. Not that it made any difference — Ian was a firm believer of whatever was put out by mainstream media.

"He's not my boyfriend, Ian," I reminded him.

Ian scoffed, "Then what's all this about?"

He held up his phone and showed me an article I'd already seen. Several of Jack's fans had sent it to me, causing me to go on a blocking rampage. The article was about Jack and Kimberly together on their newest press tour, their relationship seemingly back 'on'.

"Doesn't that upset you?"

Here we go, I thought. *It's like having an internet troll living in my house.*

"I mean, look how close he is with his ex. Aren't you just the smallest bit pissed? I'd be pulling out my hair if that were my man."

I took a deep breath. Had Jack said that he wasn't able to take on a girlfriend along with everything else right now? Yes. Was he being papped cosying up to Kimberly while away on tour? Yes. Was I pissed about it? Absolutely. Was I going to rage my feelings, throw my laptop out of the window, and let Ian know he was getting to me? Not a sodding chance.

I shrugged, "He's not my boyfriend, Ian. He can do what he wants."

"Okay, on your broken heart be it." Ian turned to leave, then remembered why he'd come in the first place. "You still didn't tell me what you wanted for dinner—"

This is why you need good friends in your life. Crap friends just flare up your anxieties for their own entertainment.

I need to move out.

1st July

No one is who they say they are. We're all just tins wearing the wrong labels. You can only know who we really are by looking inside. And there's nothing worse than finding someone who you think is a beautiful soup, is actually just rancid kidney beans.

Ian has officially pushed me over the edge. I was coping just fine until I walked into the living room and saw Jack shirtless, kissing the face off Kimberly all over the TV. Ian *CLAIMS* he was just channel-hopping, but *Violins in Vienna* isn't on regular TV, so now I feel like drowning myself in vodka.

Amarra, thankfully, agreed with my choice of coping mechanism and took me to some hip, cool bar in central London (that I most definitely didn't belong in). The people around me were glamorous, practically naked, and dripping with nightlife charisma. I was barely keeping my cocktail down.

At the bar, Amarra was getting chatted up by two different blokes. She swatted them away like flies, no doubt put off by their inadequate height. As I watched from the wall, amused, I felt an arm suddenly wrap itself around my waist.

"*Hollywood!*"

Oliver. I'd almost completely forgotten about him since our last horrendous hook-up. He smelled strongly of beer and cheap deodorant.

"Oh, God, Oliver," I shouted over the loud, thumping music. "You alright?"

"You still remember my name then?" he teased, not letting go of my waist and pressing his lips uncomfortably close to my ear lobe. "Thought you'd be too famous now."

His breath was hot and stuck to my neck.

What had I ever seen in this guy? I wondered, looking over his squeaky-clean features, his rock-solid body and too-white-to-ever-be-considered-natural teeth.

"How's Tilly?" I asked, desperately trying to change the subject and wriggle out from his hold.

"How's the boyfriend?" Oliver asked. I wasn't sure if he hadn't heard me or was just flat-out ignoring me. "Got sent those pictures of you and him outside his house a couple of times. Funny that Jack Hart's now dating my sloppy seconds."

I felt my blood begin to boil. *What did he just call me?*

"You liked me first," Oliver continued, "you've got to tell him that. You wanted me first. I remember you gagging for it when we went out for dinner that one time. Do you remember? Bet you still want it now, don't you?"

Oliver's grip on me tightened, and suddenly my anger turned to fear.

"Oliver. Let go."

"Come on, just one kiss," he whispered, going for my neck and locking me into a hold I couldn't get out of. "Or are you too famous to kiss me now?"

He planted his sweaty, alcohol-smeared lips forcefully against mine. I dropped my glass, heard it smash, and dug my nails as hard as I could into his arm. He pulled back and I managed to let out a scream.

"Oi! Wanker!" I heard Amarra suddenly yell, pulling Oliver off me.

He spun and growled at her. "Who the fuck do you think you're—"

With no hesitation, Amarra swiftly kneed him in the bollocks, and Oliver crumpled up in pain.

"There always has to be one prick that ruins it, doesn't there?" Amarra took my arm and led me to the exit, my legs barely able to keep me upright. "And just when I was starting to enjoy myself."

2nd July

Ignore the why. Ignore the why. Ignore the why.

I felt like pure and utter shit. The taste of Oliver was still on my lips, and the smell of him still on my skin, even after my third shower. I knew Oliver was what some might call '*a lad's lad*', but I never thought he'd be the kind of bloke to do something like that. Neither did Ian, who swore up and down that Amarra and I had made a mistake. Ian was closer to Tilly and her brother than we were, so it made sense he'd want to keep that friendship drama-free and pretend like he hadn't just heard Oliver had sexually assaulted me. Ian tried every excuse on Oliver's behalf that he could think of:

"He obviously had too much to drink."

"Maybe he was getting mixed signals. I mean, what were you wearing? Was it one of Amarra's dresses? You know the kind of attention she attracts."

And my personal favourite, "You have slept with him in the past, Mel. He probably just thought you were still into him."

I couldn't bear to hear any more of it and crawled into bed after calling in sick for work. I didn't know how to make this horrible, sickly feeling go away. The tighter I curled myself into a ball, the more I began to doubt myself. Did Ian have a point? Did Oliver just think I was still into him? I had slept with him twice before, and even Oliver had made a point of mentioning I'd wanted him badly at one point. If Oliver had kissed me like that a year ago, I probably would have let him. *I don't even know anymore.*

By this point it was God-knows-what o'clock in the morning. My face was red raw and tear stained. My body and mind, broken. I took a deep breath and worried that what I was feeling might never go away. The guilt, and shame, and everything else swimming around my head.

All I want is a hug.
Not from Amarra, or Ian, or my Dad... or even Jack.
I want my mum.

3rd July

Time doesn't heal or make it any better, just makes it different. Time provides distractions that fill the void and numb the pain.

I knew something was up from the moment Ian fell into my bedroom. He didn't bother knocking, just tumbled through the door frame, phone in hand and a flurry of apologies spilling out of his mouth:

"Oh, God, I'm so sorry."

He didn't leave any time for me to respond.

"This probably isn't the best way to tell you, but I don't want you to find out any other way. I'm so sorry…"

Concluding with, "Please don't freak out. It's all going to be okay, I promise."

Freak out was an odd phrase to use. *Break down. Spiral. Crash and burn. Throw yourself out the window.* Any of those would've made more sense.

Glaring back at me, on full brightness, was a blurry but still very clear photo of Oliver kissing me. I felt vomit crawl to the top of my throat as I reimagined the sensation of his hands slithering over my skin, the taste of his beer-soaked lips forced against mine.

WHEN THE BOYFRIEND'S AWAY, MELISSA WILL PLAY

The headline was horrendous — the article was even worse. I felt my eyes sting as they filled with tears. I hadn't blinked for minutes as I scanned the ever-worsening tabloid.

'An insider source has told us Hart's new girlfriend, Melissa Bishop, is already straying from her boyfriend while he's away. Jack Hart is currently in Brazil on the press tour for the upcoming season of Violins in Vienna, meanwhile Bishop is kissing her ex, Oliver Montgumary. Taken last night in—'

"They've got Oliver's name down here," I spluttered. "How do they know who Oliver is?"

"I don't know," Ian's bottom lip wobbled. He crawled into bed with me and wrapped an arm around my shoulders. "Oh, babe, I honestly don't know."

"Oh my God," I scrambled for my phone, throwing Ian off me. I didn't want to be comforted right now. I certainly didn't want to be touched. "What if Jack's seen this?!"

As I reached for my phone it started to ring.

Withheld number. That meant Jack. I answered. *God, what must he be thinking?*

A woman's voice rendered me silent.

"Miss Bishop? Hello? Is this Miss Melissa Bishop?"

If this is my dentist ringing up to change my appointment, I'm going to throw myself in front of a bus.

"Err... Yeah?"

"My name's Hannah, I'm one of the nurses here at Whittington Hospital. We've currently got Arthur West in our care and we're going to need you to come down—"

Arthur? Jack's grandad. *Why the hell are they ringing me about Arthur?*

Ian was staring at me dumbly, unaware he wasn't the only one clueless as to what the hell was going on.

"I think you've got the wrong number."

"We have a 'Melissa Bishop' down as Arthur's secondary emergency contact—"

"That's me, but I—"

"Well, I'm so sorry to have to inform you, but Mr West's taken a poor turn. The district nurses checked on him this afternoon, and found him unresponsive. We've brought him in and it doesn't look like he's going to recover from this, Miss Bishop. We're unsure of how long he has... Do you know how soon you can be here?"

I swallowed the very hard, very large lump that had lodged itself in my throat, before stupidly replying, "I'll be there as soon as I can."

There was little noise on the ward. Few staff, and even fewer patients. I'd never seen a hospital so quiet. Mum's hospital was completely the opposite. She'd been admitted twice in the nine weeks leading up to her death. The first for a supposed heart attack; then again for a real heart attack and minor stroke.

"I've got a bingo card," she told me during her second admission. "Trying to get all the mega medical problems stamped off before I kick the bucket. I've got cancer, heart attack, stroke, anaphylactic shock — I'm just waiting on pneumonia and then I can shout, '*Bingo!*' and die happy."

"Don't make jokes…" I'd warned her, sitting by her bedside. "It's not funny."

Mum pulled a face at me, then took my hand and squeezed it. "When I go, Mel. I want to go out laughing."

The nurse on reception escorted me to Arthur; I found him in a dimly lit room wired up to a million different machines. Tubes were hooked up to his wrist, nose, and several disappeared under his bedsheet. He looked nothing like he had the last time I'd seen him. There was no representation of a jolly, well-trimmed, slimmer version of Santa Claus here. Arthur's face had become gaunt, his beard slightly wild, his jaw slack and hanging unnaturally. His breathing was deep, irregular, and loud. It was almost as if he was reaching, every time, for his last breath.

I sat silently in the chair beside him and gingerly took his hand. There was near to no warmth in his skin. His wrist was heavy and limp in my hand. I squeezed it, doubtful he even knew I was there. *Why was I here?*

I'd left in such a rush, Ian too busy trying to talk to me about that bastard article, to notice I'd moved on — this was a perfectly timed distraction from having to think about it.

No, Arthur wasn't my grandad, he wasn't even someone I knew but — *if he does die while I'm out there, he's going to be completely on his own.* Jack had said those words with such pain in his voice. He'd made it clear one of his biggest fears was the prospect of Arthur dying with no one beside him.

That was a fear I never had for my mum as Dad never left her side, but that didn't mean I didn't understand it. Because, in the end, when it came down to that fateful moment, Dad wasn't in the room — he'd stepped out to make a brew.

So, in the end, it was just me and Mum. And I'm glad it had happened that way, I don't know how Dad would've coped if he'd been in my shoes watching Mum take her last breaths. It wasn't magical, or spiritual, *or funny* like I'd hoped it would be. It was traumatic, and scarring, and if I'm honest with myself, I've never gotten over it. Nobody, and nothing, prepares you for it. For how quick they turn cold. How fast they solidify, and how much their face distorts as their eyes glaze over and their jaw slackens to a point where their bottom teeth look as if they're about to fall out.

That was the final image I got of my mum. As brutal as it was, I wouldn't change it for the world because it meant she hadn't been on her own. And I wasn't prepared to let Arthur be on his own either.

"It's Melissa, Sir," I whispered, reminding myself I was here for Jack and Arthur's sake, not mine. "Jack's friend. I've just come to sit with you for a little while, is that okay?"

There was no response. Just endless, empty silence, and then a strained, raspy gasp for air.

"I'm sorry if I'm intruding," I began, not really knowing why I was talking at all. I think because I was nervous. Terrified I was making a huge mistake, and taking one massive, insensitive step in the wrong direction. "Just thought you might want some company while you wait..."

Wait for what? I thought. For death to appear with a big scythe? Or one of God's angels with a 'Get into Heaven card'? Or nothing? I had no idea what this man believed in.

A nurse came in, a student scuttling behind him. "Oh, hello," he said, straightened. "We didn't know you were in here. I'm so sorry."

I shook my head, still holding Arthur's limp hand tightly, "It's fine. I don't mind."

The nurse smiled sympathetically and looked over Arthur's notes, the student barely making eye contact. The lack of conversation made me very aware of how dire Arthur's condition was. They were clearly under instruction not to speak unless spoken to.

"Have you had any luck getting in contact with his next of kin?" I finally asked, unable to take the nagging in my head, or the uncomfortable silence any longer.

The nurse gave me a quizzical look. "You're Mr West's next of kin, aren't you?"

I shook my head. "The woman on the phone said I was *second* or something. I don't even know what that means."

After a short whisper in her ear, the student hurried out of the room. The nurse stood flicking through more of Arthur's notes. "We've got all your information here. Melissa Bishop. For status, they've written... Visiting?" There was a literal scratch of the head. "*Visiting?* Why the hell have they written 'visiting'?"

Then it hit me. The form I'd been handed the last time I'd come to see Arthur. It wasn't a visiting questionnaire at all. It was a contact sheet.

"What's your relation to the patient?"

"Grand-daughter," I lied, panicking that if I gave the truthful answer they'd throw me out.

The nurse scribbled across the paper just as the student came back into the room. "They can't get past the first ring," she squeaked, still not making eye contact with me. "Reception can keep trying, but it keeps going straight to voicemail."

"Okay..." I trailed off. "Thank you."

They both left. The room returned to its eerie, unnatural silence. I wanted to speak to Arthur, bring him words of comfort, but I had nothing. I was drawing up a complete and utter blank, second-guessing whether I should have come at all.

4th July

Some friends are like flies — they only hang around when there's shit going on.

Mum was transferred to a hospice when she got too ill to be in the hospital. She didn't want to be there, she wanted to be at home. I tried to visit everyday with Dad, but we found she got overwhelmed when both of us arrived. So, we decided to go separately. With Dad, Mum was positive, upbeat, adamant she was going to be a medical marvel, and she would be back and fighting fit in no time. With me, she was slightly more... *realistic.*

"Don't let anybody come to my funeral that I wouldn't want there," she said, staring out of the hospice window. "I'd rather the crematorium be empty than filled with people I don't like, and I *know* don't like me."

"It won't be empty," I reassured. "I'm definitely going, and Dad's RSVP'd as a 'maybe'—"

Mum laughed, it swiftly mutated into uncontrollable coughs. She held a tissue close to her mouth, letting it be speckled with blood. "Your jokes are going to kill me one day," she croaked. Her eyes crinkled at the corners as she smiled, but they all swiftly vanished when she noticed I was silently crying.

"What's wrong?" she asked, dumbly.

"I don't — I just don't think I'm ready. The world isn't going to be a world I recognise when you..."

Mum's eyebrows furrowed. "This is one of your things, isn't it? That, because I'm in it, the world is a certain way. And it's going to go *pfft* because I'm not."

I felt myself start to sob. A timid "yeah" fluttered out of my mouth.

It was true. The world was going to completely change the moment my mum left it. I had never gone a single day without her. She was my everything. She had grown me, raised me, helped me, and was now leaving me — unequipped to spend the rest of my life without her.

Mum smiled at me sympathetically, and let out a half bemused laugh. "I'm not that special, actually, to tilt the world on its axis."

"Mum," I assured her sternly, "you really are. You are to *me*."

She laughed weakly, flattered at the sentiment but still not acknowledging that I meant every word. My world was going to end with her death. I just knew it.

"You'll be fine, Mel. I know you will."

"And what if I'm not?"

I awoke to something worse than nothingness. Complete and utter nothingness, thrown in with near-enough pitch blackness and a hand clutching mine that wasn't my mum's. Arthur's eyes were the only thing glistening in the dark — wide and staring at the ceiling. My heart fell right to the pit of my stomach. I searched for the nurses' button and pressed it as hard as I could, never letting go of Arthur's hand.

No one came.

Arthur's eyes flickered my way, his head frozen solid into his pillow. He made a groan that I could've sworn sounded like... "Josie?"

I swallowed.

Arthur gripped harder onto my hand, it no doubt taking every last ounce of strength he had left. My heart broke for him. He really thought, in his final moments, I was his daughter.

His hand then went limp, and I could see the shine in his eyes begin to drain away.

Nurses came flurrying in, seconds too late. Not that there was anything they could have done. Reality seemed to blur, as they flocked around me. Going about their work, doing what needed to be done. The only one who approached me was the student nurse from before. She took my hand, sat beside me, and smiled as sympathetically as she could. I hadn't realised it, but I was crying. Silently sobbing for a man I didn't even know.

The student nurse hadn't really left my side since they'd quietly whisked Arthur away and off the ward. As she handed me a scolding cup of tea, in a tiny plastic cup, she said, "I'm sorry for your loss."

It wasn't my loss. I wanted to tell her. I hadn't lost anything — Jack had, and he didn't even know it.

She finally left me when Amarra called. We exchanged a few words. I explained: Yes, I was at the hospital. Yes, I was okay. No, there was nothing I needed.

"Does Jack know?" she asked.

No, Jack was no doubt still living in ignorant bliss, thousands of miles away, on a white, sandy, Brazilian beach, reading about my alleged affair with Oliver.

"No, they've tried to call him but Jack's phone keeps— "

As if the universe was playing some cruel trick, my words had seemingly summoned the man himself. Jack came bolting through the ward doors on the other end of the corridor; a platinum blonde woman following sluggishly behind.

"Can I call you back?" I whispered.

"Why? Is everything okay?"

"Yeah," I lied, "Jack's here."

I hung up before Amarra had a chance to respond and withdrew into the back of my chair, wanting to blend into the wall as much as possible.

"We're here to see Arthur West," Jack said, approaching the reception desk. His voice was a little panicked. He looked drained and defeated. "I tried ringing him yesterday but there was no answer, so I rang here and they said he was on this ward. Is he — is he okay?"

Jesus Christ.

Could he see me? Did I want him to see me? It's not like I could head for the exit, Jack was right by the door. Despite being on the third floor, the window looked appealing...

"Could you repeat the name of the person you're here to see, please?"

The woman beside him leaned across the desk, readjusting the garish handbag on her shoulder. "For God's sake, he started with that! Arthur West. I tell you, you lot are bloody hopeless."

"Don't start, Mum," Jack snapped, before apologising on her behalf.

The now scowling receptionist went back to tapping away on her computer, before her face completely changed. Her scowl faded away and she looked up at Jack sympathetically. "I'm... If you just give me a moment to grab one of the doctors, I'll be right back."

As soon as she was gone, Jack's mum groaned loudly into her hands.

"This is such a waste of time, Jacko!" she grumbled. "The geezer isn't even going to know who I am."

"He's got cancer, Mum, not dementia," Jack rolled his eyes, and I tried desperately to stay out of his line of sight. I'd decided he didn't need to know I was here, it would only make everything worse.

A doctor I didn't recognise came round the corner, the receptionist on her heels. The doctor extended her hand towards Jack, introducing herself as Doctor Shaw.

"Jack Hart," he replied, taking her hand and shaking it slowly.

"And I'm Josie West, not that anybody seems to care," Jack's mum chimed in.

"We've been trying to get a hold of you..." Shaw continued, unfazed.

Jack pulled out his phone, "Sorry, I've had to use a different number while I've been away. It completely slipped my mind to let you know as I was speaking to Grandad most days anyway. How's he doing?"

I shouldn't be here. I internally screamed, feeling trapped by the scolding cup of tea in my hands, and Jack blocking my exit route. Then it occurred to me — this Shaw was about to tell them Arthur had died, but she wouldn't do it here. No, she would take them into a side room and let them down easy. *So all I have to do is stay as still as possible until they're whisked off, and then bolt for the door.* Not a solid plan, but the best one I'd got.

"I'm sorry to inform you both, but Arthur passed away this morning."

Well, that's that plan fucked.

I could feel the atmosphere of the whole corridor thicken. Jack's mum let out a half laugh, half blub of horror.

"You're joking?" she said, trying desperately to make light of what would be a very sick joke. "Tell me you're kidding. He was fine the other day. Jacko, you said he was fine!"

There was no response from Jack. Out of the corner of my eye, I could see his whole body had gone stiff, his eyes fixed on Shaw.

"We've moved him downstairs. If you would still like to see him, I can have one of the nurses escort you down and answer any questions you have—"

"Downstairs?" Jack's mum's eyes widened. "As in the *morgue?* You want me to go into a basement full of dead people? Are you *mad*?"

The doctor took a notably deep breath, "I know this is very difficult news for you, Ms West. We will try and make you as comfortable as possible. We'll be able to place him in a side room—"

"No!" she yelped. "No, absolutely not. Not happening!"

Shaw gave the receptionist a brief sideways glance before turning her attention to Jack, who was still frozen to the spot. I wanted to jump out of my chair, run and hug him. Hold him, tell him everything was going to be alright — despite the fact I knew the world as he knew it was currently imploding.

"Was he...?" Jack whispered under his breath, slowly trying to find his voice. "Was Grandad on his own when it happened? Or was a nurse with him or something?"

"I believe his grand-daughter was with him."

My stomach felt like it was going to drop out of my arse.

Jack's mum let out a bitter laugh. "Well, now I know you're having us on. *A grand-daughter?* He doesn't have one. Two grandsons only, Doc."

"She was his secondary emergency contact. We have her on file."

Definitely time to exit via the window, I thought, placing my tea under the chair and grabbing my coat, getting ready to run.

"Oh yeah?" Jack's mum laughed again. "What's her name?"

The receptionist, who'd returned to her desk, began typing away.

"We have a... *Melissa Bishop*?"

I wanted the ground to swallow me up.

Jack's mum scoffed. "Never heard of her."

Jack suddenly began scrambling for his phone, patting down his coat and trouser pockets. "She was here?"

"Oh, you know her, do you? Got a sister I don't know about?" Jack's mum rolled her eyes. "I gave birth a third time and have just happened to forget, did I? What sick joke are you all trying to play on me today?"

Jack held his phone to his ear and my heart stopped as the ringtone from my pocket began to echo down the corridor. I saw Jack's eyes glaring at me from around Shaw, his face unreadable. He hung up and began charging towards me. I felt like a red flag being waved in front of a rabid bull.

"What the hell are you doing here?" he growled.

From the rage behind his eyes I could instantly tell Jack had seen and read the article. The fury in his voice wasn't just heightened due to Arthur — this was personal.

I jumped up, hands out in surrender. "Jack, I'm so sorry," I began, with no idea what I could say to justify any of this. What did he think of me? What could I have possibly said to make any of this better? I couldn't bring up Oliver and explain. I couldn't bring up Arthur and apologise, I just needed to get out of there, and fast.

"They called, and I didn't think. I'm just— I'm so sorry, I had no right to be—"

"No, you didn't," he snapped, his mum now approaching from behind.

"Is this the daughter I don't know about?"

"She's no one," Jack hissed over his shoulder.

I felt my eyes burn.

No one.

I'm. No. One.

"You said you were afraid he'd be on his own while you were away. I was just—" I breathed, "I was just trying to help."

I began walking, then running, for the exit. No one followed me.

Thank God.

Ian could do nothing but hold me as I sobbed. Amarra was lurking by the kitchen door, biting her nails.

"God, you ain't half had a ride of it," Ian tried to joke. No one laughed. "I haven't had this much trouble with a bloke since I was at uni and were dating that Younis fella."

"Ian, will you just knock it on the head?" Amarra snapped before turning back to me. "I'll whack the kettle on."

Ian audibly scoffed. "God, she's had her knickers in a right twist since you got home." He began to stroke my head; whether he was trying to be comforting, or was just bothered by my frizz itching his face, I wasn't sure. "I don't know why she's the one who's worked up. I'm the one who's been left in the dark all morning. At least she was getting regular updates—"

"What are you chatting about?" I blubbed, pulling away from him. "We only spoke for about two seconds this morning. She's been as much in the dark as you have."

I reached for a tissue and dabbed my red-raw face. Ian was now scowling at me.

"I know she's your preferred friend, Mel. You don't have to lie to me."

I couldn't help but let out an exhausted laugh. Now was *so* not the time for Ian to start waffling about his friendship insecurities.

"I'm not lying," I reassured him, cupping his face, and letting out another weak sob. Despite him being a terrible housemate sometimes and touch-and-go friend, I did love him.

Amarra returned, balancing three cups of tea on a wooden chopping board. "You're out of sugar."

"Who've you been on the phone with all morning?" Ian asked sharply.

Amarra blanked. "What?"

I ignored them both and curled up on the sofa, grabbing a blanket. I felt too sorry for myself to deal with their petty arguments and weird disagreements right now. I felt sure neither of them would have noticed if I just slipped upstairs and cried for the next twenty four hours.

"This morning. You said you were on the phone with Mel the whole time, but she's now saying it was two seconds max. So, which is it?"

"Why does it matter?" I asked, only then noticing Amarra's jaw was clenched and she was visibly shaking.

Ian rose off the sofa, towering over Amarra, "Because she's done nothing but talk about Jack and his Grandad this morning. So if she weren't talking to you about it, who *were* she talking to?"

Amarra looked like a rabbit caught in the headlights.

A sick feeling began to bubble in the pit of my stomach. I swallowed hard. "...*Amarra?*"

It was like time suddenly slowed as she looked me dead in the face. Her eyes filled with fear. In those milliseconds, I began to notice everything I hadn't before. I'd been so caught up in my own crappy circle of chaos I hadn't noticed the new nails, new phone and case, the haircut, the eyelash extensions, everything *new.*

I pulled out my phone and scrolled the internet looking for the article of Oliver and me. I found it, the photo bringing vomit to my mouth. The angle of the camera, the position the photographer must have been in to get that shot. They would've had to have been standing at the bar... *right where Amarra had been.*

'*Insider source*'. The two words leapt out at me, and I felt myself burning up.

"You did this?" I spun my phone around.

"Mel, I can explain— "

"*You did this*!" I screamed.

All the pieces started to come together like some twisted puzzle. "This isn't the first time, is it? The photographers outside Jack's house — you were the only person who knew I was there. *Oh, God* — have you sent these reporters to the hospital?"

Amarra's silence and trembling bottom lip confirmed what I'd hoped she would deny.

"He's just lost his grandad — how can you be so *heartless?*"

Ian couldn't stand any longer, his jaw agape. He fell back onto the sofa, meanwhile Amarra was running her fingers through her freshly cut and coloured hair.

"You have no idea what it's like, Mel," she sucked her teeth and glared at me. "I don't come from a rich family like you. You claim you're broke, but you've got your daddy in a villa ready to cover any rent payment that may have been missed. You have *money,* whether it's directly in your account or not. I don't. No one in my family does. If I miss a payment, I'm out. Sofa surfing. Living with nothing and no one to help me. They offered me thousands, Mel. More and more every time. I couldn't say no. I didn't have a choice. It isn't because I don't love you. It isn't because I don't care, it was because it was the smart thing to do!" she snapped. "A few pictures, a few bits of information, about a guy you're always saying doesn't care about you! So it doesn't matter. None of it matters, especially when the next day's clickbait comes out and everyone's moved on to the next load of tripe gossip. You've got a thick skin, I knew it wouldn't even affect you, and Jack's probably used to this by now."

I had no words.

No response.

Nothing.

Ian, however, immediately launched for her. "Are you *kidding* me?!" he screamed, almost lunging across the coffee table. "Do you hear yourself, Mar? I like a good bit of gossip between friends, but I would never, *ever* sell out my friend's private life. No matter what they were offering!"

"Five thousand quid, Ian," Amarra snarled. "That pays for my rent for six months."

"And loses you your best friends," Ian pointed at the door. "Get the fuck out. Now."

"Mel," Amarra turned her attention back to me, "you have to at least see where I'm coming from."

I did see where she was coming from. I truly did.

"I said get out!"

"I wasn't talking to you, Ian!" Amarra swept up my hands in hers, her eyes pleading and desperate. I'd never seen her like this. "Mel, you can take a cut, if that makes you feel better about it! Hell, have Oliver's cut, he'll understand—"

My breath hitched, my vision starting to blur.

Wait. "What?"

"He's proper pissed at me because I kneed him, but I told him he took it too far! He was only supposed to kiss you for a split—"

"You *planned* for Oliver to attack me?"

"No, I—" Amarra blinked, thinking back, realising what she'd let slip. "We just thought—"

Jack had warned me about this. Thinking about it now, it's almost like he prophesied it. 'It's always the people you least expect who stab you in the back the fastest and the deepest.

I pulled my hands free from Amarra's grasp, slowly. "You heard what Ian said," I hissed. "*Get out.*"

5th July

Just because you want it more than anything, doesn't mean it's yours. Auditions are a prime example of that. Doesn't matter how talented you are, or how famous you get, some roles are just not meant to be.

Sleep had almost become like a foreign concept. I spent most, if not all, of the night refreshing an internet search of Jack's name, waiting for the inevitable publication. Surprisingly, it never came. Ian had turned feral. He was more distraught by Amarra's betrayal than I was. I think that's because I was still somewhat in shock. Ian had fully accepted what Amarra had done, and begun his rage rampage over it. I was still waiting for one of them to tell me it was all just a prank. Ian was reigning *Mr Blabbermouth,* it's true, but he was harmless. What Amarra had done, her justifications aside, had broken me.

    I checked my phone: *03:26am.* I clambered out of bed, and pulled on my nearest coat and trainers, all the while thinking, *now is as good a time as any, and probably the best chance I've got.*

The deep hum of the taxi driving off eventually dimmed, leaving me in complete silence, staring up at Jack's front door. I approached, knowing this was the wrong thing to do, but aware this was the only option I had. I rang the doorbell and waited. In my head, I imagined Jack to be fast asleep in his bed, but surprisingly that wasn't the case at all.

A very dishevelled and confused Jack peered around the doorframe after only a minute or two.

"Mel?" he croaked. "What the hell are you doing here?"

He opened the door fully, revealing he was still wearing the same clothes I'd seen him in at the hospital.

"I need to talk to you," my voice trembled.

"Do you know what time it is?"

"It's important," I breathed.

After a moment of heightened tension between us, he reluctantly opened the door and let me over the threshold.

In the kitchen, I saw Jack had an array of paperwork strewn across the breakfast table. Stacks of old photographs, newspaper articles, vintage theatre programmes.

"You'll have to keep it quiet and make it quick, my mum's asleep in the room above us," Jack said, his eyes notably glancing at the ceiling. He leaned against the counter furthest away from me and folded his arms across his chest. "So, what is it?"

"Umm," I stalled. I wasn't sure where I was even supposed to begin. "A few things really. Firstly, I wanted to apologise for being at the hospital yesterday."

Jack's eyes narrowed.

"Honestly, I wasn't thinking. The hospital called, saying they couldn't get a hold of you and I knew you wanted—"

"Since when have you cared about what I want?" Jack cut me off.

My eyes widened. That wasn't a question I'd prepared an answer for.

I've always cared, I thought. *I thought that was obvious.*

Jack slid his phone across the breakfast table separating us — the photo of Oliver seemingly holding me in a twisted embrace stared back at me.

"And you have the balls to say I'm playing games?"

Just seeing Oliver with his hands all over me brought back the stench of his rancid deodorant. My cheeks burned as my eyes began to fill. "It's not what you think—"

"Don't even start, Mel," Jack barked. His harshness was understandable, but it still stung like hell. It reminded me of when I first met him. A bloke full of buried pain, with a standoff attitude. Before, it had pissed me off. Now it just broke my heart. "It's always something! Always some bloody excuse or another. You were too drunk to remember kissing me in Manchester, you were 'playing along' in France, you thought I didn't like you despite the fact I've done nothing but tell you that I do — and when I think we're finally on the same page, you pull out this shit!"

I couldn't look up at him. I didn't know what else to say other than the plain and simple truth. "I was being assaulted."

Saything those four words opened up the floodgates. I began to silently sob. It was as if the realisation and weight of what had happened to me was hitting me all over again.

"...What?"

I finally looked up, and through a filter of tears I saw Jack staring at me, his arms now limp by his sides. "It was a setup. Oliver—" saying his name almost made me wretch, I could feel his fingers digging into my sides, his breath on my neck. "He's just some guy I hooked up with who wanted thirty seconds of fame, and decided to attack me while my supposed best friend took pictures."

Jack blinked, absorbing it all.

"Amarra took the photos and sold them. She's been selling information for weeks, maybe months. I honestly don't know." I scrunched up my nose. It was taking everything I had not to have a full-on breakdown. "I thought she was my friend, Jack..."

Jack didn't speak, silence consuming us both. I couldn't look at him any longer, it was too painful. I couldn't read his face at all, could only speculate what he was thinking of this entire situation. And most importantly what he was thinking of me.

"What kind of information?" he finally asked.

"Everything worth anything," I confessed with a sniffle. "She's told them all about us... And your grandad."

Jack's eyes glanced over all the documents strewn across the breakfast table between us. "Is that why there were photographers at the hospital today?"

I nodded, "Amarra knew you were there, I was on the phone with her just as you came on the ward. About an hour after— "

The mere attempt at mentioning Arthur's death sent Jack hurtling forward. He grabbed hold of a couple of papers, and held them as if tempted to launch them across the kitchen.

"So instead of getting this obituary I've been trying to piece together, my grandad instead gets a front-page exclusive?!"

"I'm so sorry, Jack. If I'd known Amarra was anything like this, I never would have said a word. I had no idea—"

"No, you never do!" Jack shouted, clearly no longer caring about waking his mum. "You overthink all the time but not one intelligent, clear thought goes through that head," he collapsed into the chair closest to him, defeated. "Naive as ever, Mel."

After a moment's silence Jack finally looked up at me, his own eyes filled with unshed tears.

"I'm sorry," Jack finally whispered. "I'm sorry for what Oliver did to you. I'm sorry for what Amarra did to you and I'm sorry for what I've done to you because if it wasn't for me, none of this would have ever happened. You'd be so much better off if you'd never met me."

My breath hitched, and I swear I felt my heart begin to tear in two.

"Don't say that," I took a nervous step towards him, trying to stop the continuous flow of silent tears.

"It's true isn't it?" Jack shrugged. "You wouldn't have gone through any of this. You wouldn't have been put through all that and seeing my—" Jack scrunched up his face, before wiping one of his cheeks with his sleeve. "Was he okay, in the end, or was he—?" Jack finally broke down, his sobs echoing around the room.

I tumbled across the kitchen and gripped Jack's face in my hands. I knew this, I recognised this. All the grief, and pain in its purest form. *The world as he knew it, ended.*

"Your grandad was at peace, Jack," I cried along with him, our foreheads touching. I felt his shaking body reverberate through mine. Both of us spiralling into our own little world. "He left with a squeeze of my hand."

"I should have stayed," Jack wept, burying his wet face into the crook of my neck. "I shouldn't have left him, I should have stayed and been there when he died. He needed me, and I deserted—"

I allowed Jack to collapse into me, taking us both to the floor. His entire weight pressed against me, his body rendered useless by the grief.

I don't know how long we stayed like that for. Melted into one another. Time seemed to pass effortlessly as Jack cried till there was absolutely nothing left.

Jack made coffee in silence. I hovered by the doorway, unsure if I'd outstayed my welcome. We hadn't spoken a word since we'd helped each other up from the floor. I'd checked the clock on the oven, it was nearing seven.

Jack's mum will be waking up soon, I thought, my eyes flicking up towards the ceiling.

Jack had once again seemingly read my mind. "Mum doesn't usually get out of bed till ten, you're fine."

I was settled to see him take two mugs out of the cupboard. One purple, one red.

As he poured the coffee our phones seemed to go off in sync. Mine ringing in my back pocket, his lighting up on the table. I checked my phone while he checked his. Ian was calling me.

"It's my publicist..." Jack said, nervously.

We both knew what it meant. The article was up.

"Do you want me to answer?" He asked, both phones ringing out.

I shrugged. This was essentially brand new territory for me.

The kitchen went back to silence as both phones went unanswered.

A notification came up on my phone. Ian had sent the link through. My thumb hovered above it. *How bad could it be?* I thought, trying my best to convince myself this would all be fine.

Jack was suddenly next to me, holding onto my wrist tightly, stopping me from clicking. "We both know reading that article, and everything that comes with it, isn't good for you," he breathed deeply. "I can't be the reason you get hurt again…"

He looked right into my eyes and I felt my heart drop as I realised what he was saying.

This was over. Us, existing in each other's lives — it had well and truly come to an end.

I had been right all along. Jack's way of life, his prime-time seat in the public eye, came with so much I couldn't handle. As long as Jack was *Jack Hart,* he wasn't for me, and I wasn't for him. I couldn't support him, and he wouldn't be able to protect me.

We both heard the heavy footsteps come stomping down the stairs.

"Jacko!" his mum called from the hallway. "Jacko, have you seen this?" The kitchen door flung open, Josie entering like a crack of thunder. Her eyes were too glued to her phone to notice I was even in the room. "Your brother just called, sent over this rubbish about your grandad! I thought you were doing some theatre, heart-felt, lovey-dovey crap? So, what the hell is this?" She finally looked up, her phone outstretched towards us both. Her face instantly fell. "Who the hell are you?"

I blinked, swallowing the ball of hard saliva in my throat. "No one. Jack, I better go."

Josie blocked my exit. "You're that girl from the hospital," she looked back at her phone. "You're *this* girl!"

My eyes couldn't help but scan the bright screen being shoved in my face.

JACK HART-BROKEN OVER FAMILY TRAGEDY AND DISASTROUS LOVE LIFE

Every inch of my body started to tremble. The air in the kitchen had become unbearably thin. I couldn't breathe.

"What the hell is she doing in your house?" Josie barked, pushing past me, and almost launching me into the fridge. "My dad's, *your grandad's,* memory has been made all about her — you know that right? She needs to leave."

"I was just leaving," I admitted, turning for one last look at Jack. I smiled at him, his mum's rants and raves becoming muffled background noise. "Bye, Jack."

I turned, Jack's parting words, "Good luck with everything, Mel," practically following me out of the door.

One Year On

Appreciating life choices, such as quitting the acting industry and instead becoming a successful and happy writer.

Ian was by the cloakroom desk, waving two programmes in his hands enthusiastically.

"Look at you!" he squealed, taking in my tan, my new dress and my chic, wheely suitcase. He hauled it over the cloakroom desk and passed the boy in the red waistcoat a fiver. "Thought you'd have a lot more luggage. You're here for a month, aren't you?"

"Save money by only doing carry-on. Plus you still have our washing machine, don't you?"

"Yeah, that now makes your clothes smell like cat piss." Ian jumped giddily, before wrapping me in a long overdue embrace. "Come on then, give us a squeeze! I've missed you."

"Yeah?" I was out of breath, the walk from Waterloo Station had been an absolute killer in heels. I felt like I had shin splints just from crossing the road before the little man turned red. "Not been too shagged up to notice I'd gone?"

"Pfft. Callum's good but he's not *that good*. Your dad doing alright?"

"Yeah, think he was glad to see the back of me after almost a year."

"Doubt that's true," Ian cupped my face in his hands and pecked a kiss on my cheek. "God, it's just so good to see you. I can't believe how well you look!" He fanned both programmes in my face. "And this is so exciting! Look at this name, see this name?" he ran his finger underneath the title. "'Written by *Melissa Bishop*!" Ian squealed. "That's you, baby!" He pointed at the top of my head and turned to the queue of people waiting to check in their coats. "This is her! Playwright extraordinaire!"

"*Ladies and gentleman, please take your seats as this evening's performance of Waiting for Monday is about to begin.*"

"So, are you excited to see this?" Ian asked, squeezing down the aisle to our seats.

I shrugged, playing it as cool as I could manage. Internally I was spiralling. When the play was finished it had been shipped off and became someone else's baby. I'd had no involvement in anything from the moment it was bought. No say in the cast, the set, the direction, the sales — not a thing. In a way, it was comforting. If it was terrible, I wouldn't be solely to blame. *Nice.*

Ian placed his arm around the back of my chair and gave me another tight squeeze. "Will you stop looking so terrified, Mel? This is going to be awesome. Everyone has been raving about it. Tilly even posted how good it was after she came here with Amarra last week. And we both know that's saying something."

Amarra.

I swallowed a hard lump in my throat. I knew it was inevitable that she would be brought up at some point. I just wasn't expecting it to be so soon. "I didn't think they'd even know I had a play on."

Ian rolled his eyes. "Of course they do! Everyone who follows me does! I'm basically your one-man promotional team at this point."

"So, Amarra and Tilly..."

Ian released his arm from around me, and began fanning himself with his programme, the theatre becoming increasingly warm with the ever-growing audience. "Oh yeah, BFFs. Who'd have thought it, ey?"

I cleared my throat, my curiosity getting the better of me. "And Amarra? Do you still talk to her?"

Ian rolled his eyes. "What do you think?"

I shrugged. I genuinely didn't know. Ian and Amarra had been close before it all kicked off. Then I left. How was I supposed to know whether they carried on playing besties while I was away?

"Well, I blocked her on pretty much everything like the day you left. But then she tried reaching out a few times on different accounts, and through Tilly and that. I hope it's okay with you, but I took it upon myself to just tell her to go fuck herself. And she must've done, because I haven't heard from her since. Anyway, enough about her. We're focusing on you tonight—"

The lights began to dim. Ian squeezed my hand, the look on his face wild with delight and pride. "Oh my god, it's starting!" he squealed under his breath as a petit actress walked on stage with a chair. She placed it centre stage, sat in it, ran her fingers through her hair, and began;

"I'm not a good person," I confess to my mum, who now no longer has the strength to lift up her head.
She smiles softly. "I don't think anyone is," she says, "not really."
The doctors said she had three to twelve months left to live. We got nine weeks."

"*Elle?*" A voice called from the wings. My eyes shot to stage left as my heart lurched forward.

I knew that voice.

"Elle, it's freezing out here. Come back inside where it's warm."

An actor dressed all in black stepped on stage and I could feel Ian tense in his chair beside me.

It was him. Really him. Not on a screen, or on the side of a bus, or even a fantasy in my mind. It was really him.

Jack.

"Do you want to leave?" Ian leaned into me as soon as the house lights raised for the interval. "Because we can—"

"I'm fine, honestly," I lied, fanning myself with the programme I'd practically scrunched to death.

"I didn't know he was in it. I didn't even know he did theatre!" Ian flicked through his programme, completely unaware people were trying to get past. "Tilly didn't say a word! Why the bloody hell didn't she tell me? Do you know what? It might not even be him."

Ian began flicking through his programme.

It is. That voice lived in my head all day, every day. Memories played from what felt like a different life, on constant repeat.

"Yeah, see? It's not him," Ian almost sounded disappointed.

"What?"

Ian held up the centrefold. Jack's headshot was smiling back at me, the name beside him, "Jack West."

"He must have a doppelganger." Ian sunk back into his chair, satisfied. "They don't half look alike."

Yeah, but they couldn't be more different, I thought.

"I thought we were heading for cocktails?" Ian pouted, throwing a thumb back to the direction of the bar.

My arm was linked with his, purely to stop myself from collapsing.

"Just walk this way a sec..."

"What for? I see no Cosmos. I see no Mojitos or Caribbean Dreams!"

My case wheels stopped turning and Ian jolted to a halt. The stage door swung open and rosy-cheeked cast members came flurrying out.

"Are you wanting your programme signed?" Ian teased, squeezing my arm. "Weirdo. You wrote the damn thing. You should be signing their programmes!" He took my case. "You do you, boo. I'll go get us a table and a round of very overpriced drinks, and I'll see you in a sec, okay?"

"Okay."

Ian tottered off back the way we came while I turned back to the stage door. The cast had all dispersed. *God, this is stupid.*

It had been months. Months and months. Jack probably wouldn't even remember me, *or he would* and in some way that made me feel worse.

The door opened with a clunk and I held my breath. Dark brunette, flowing hair made my heart sink. Not Jack, just the lead actress of the play, happy with her headphones in and sweatpants on. She smiled awkwardly at me, hesitantly removing a pod from her ear.

"You okay there?"

I nodded, scrunching the programme in my sweaty palms to a pulp.

"Yeah, just waiting for someone..."

"Yeah? Is it Oscar? He said his girlfriend was coming tonight."

"Err, no," my blood was running so hot I could feel my heartbeat in my ears. "I'm a friend of Jack's."

"Oh."

I chewed my cheek so hard I thought it might bleed. "Is he still in there?"

The brunette smiled, nodded and put her pod back in her ear. "Yeah. He's always the last one out so you might be waiting a while."

Minutes felt like hours. Cold breezes were light relief from the ever rising temperature of my skin. *If I wait any longer I'm either going to freeze to death or melt into a puddle.*

Ian must have been drinking himself into a stupor by now.

Clunk.

The stage door swung open and Jack came falling through it with his duffle bag tangled around the handle.

"Let go, you prick."

Jack's eyes flickered up at me. The colour of his pupils, just as green and as rich as I remembered. He finally freed his bag strap, his cheeks notably flushed, then patted down his jeans. "Sorry, this door is temperamental."

"Maybe it just has a bit of an attitude."

Jack froze. His eyes fixated on his jeans until his shoulders tensed up and his head rose slowly. His eyes came level with mine. I gave an awkward sort of half-wave, my palms now layered with sweat. I'd played this scenario in my head so many times, rehearsed what I would say, if by some chance Jack and I ever did meet again, and yet, now we were face to face, I couldn't even croak a 'Hello'.

"Don't say you've forgotten who I am again," Jack chuckled nervously, taking a step towards me and outstretching his hand, "it's Jack."

I smiled and shook it, "Nice to meet you, Jack."

THE END

Special Acknowledgements.
My Cheerleaders

My fiancé, Jamie and our beautiful daughter. My gorgeous, supportive family. (Dad got the shout out at the start but I'll put him here as well). So, Dad, *again*. My sisters, Esther & Zoë. My bonus family, Rachel, Alan, Grace and Rose.

My glorious friends, Paige, Rhys, Emmy, Mandy, Annie, Jimmy, Cris, Bella, Rach, Rupert, Alys, Martin & Gill.

My agents Oliver, Natalie, Humphrey and Ruby.

The doggos Bumble and Rubble.

And of course… Mum.

The support squad is endless, I could go on but fearful of the word count. I'm so very lucky and blessed to have each and every one of you in my life. Thank you for the unwavering support, the pick-ups when I've been down, and grounding me when I've spiralled up too high.

Without you I wouldn't be here.

Cheers.

Author Bio

Megan Parkinson is an English actor best known for her performance as Sam Murgatroyd in *Ackley Bridge*. Growing up in West Yorkshire, surrounded by her mad, loving family, Megan eventually moved to London, aged 18, to pursue her dream of being an actor. There she trained with the *National Youth Theatre Rep Company*, before signing with *Independent Talent Group Ltd* and working on shows such as *Game of Thrones, C.B. Strike,* and *Harlots*.

In September 2020, Megan's mother, Fiona, was diagnosed with stage four breast cancer. Despite filming her final season with *Ackley Bridge* at the time, Megan was still, thankfully, able to be with her mother when she eventually passed away, at home, in November 2020.

Three years after her mother's passing, now a mother herself, Megan was inspired to pick up her diaries from her time living in London, and her mother's end-of-life care, and use them as the foundations for *Melodramatic* and the upcoming prequel, *Waiting for Monday*.

Melodramatic is Megan Parkinson's first published novel.

Printed in Great Britain
by Amazon